To Dan Ryan,
Happy Birthday with the
best wishes of Harvey and Vera!

Judy Bond Hanson

Spirit of the Winding Water

SPIRIT OF
THE WINDING
WATER

An Exposition-Lochinvar Book

A Novel
of the
Epic 1877 Wilderness Flight
of the Nez Perce Indians

JUDY BOND HANSON

Exposition Press   Hicksville, New York

For Jay, with love

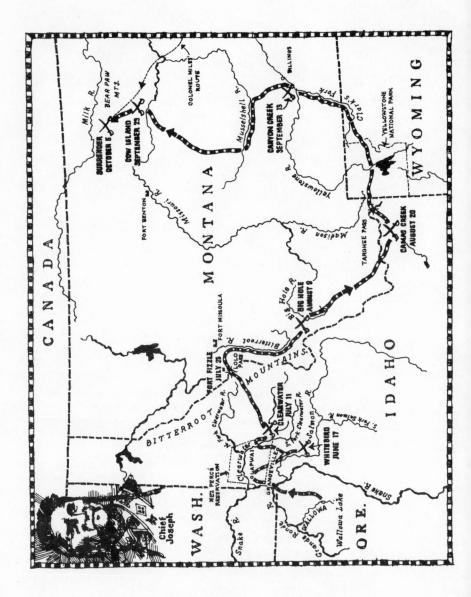

NEZ PERCE TERMS

Ahkunkenekoo. Land Above
Asotins. Looking Glass' band of Nez Perce
Chuslum Mox Mox. Yellow Bull
Heinmot Tooyalaket. Thunder Rolling in the Mountains
  (Chief Joseph)
Hohots. Grizzly bear
Hunyewat. Deity
Imnaha. Northeast Oregon river, tributary to Snake
Iskumtselalik Pah. Place of the Ground Squirrels
Kahmuenem. Snake River
Kamisnim Takin. Camas Meadows
Kopluts. War club
Lamtamas. White Bird's band of Nez Perce
Mahsamyetten. Buzzard Mountain
Meopkowit. Baby
Nasook Nema. Salmon Creek
Numipu. The People
Sapachesap. Cave on Cottonwood Creek
Shoyapee. White man
Taz alago. Good-by
Tekash. Cradleboard
Tepahlewam. Ancient Nez Perce camp near Lapwai
Tewat. Medicine man
Toma Alwawinmi. Springtime, Joseph's wife
Tasanim Alikos Pah. Place of the Manure Fire
Wallamwatkins. Joseph's band of Nez Perce
Wyakin. Personal attending spirit

"Nez Percé (French, literally, pierced nose) 1: a member of an Amerindian people of Idaho, Washington, and Oregon. 2: a language of the Nez Percé people."—*Webster's New Collegiate Dictionary*.

Although Webster preserves the accent on the final e of Percé, it does not acknowledge that the e is ever pronounced in standard American. The name of the tribe, among the Nez Perces themselves and their neighbors in the northwestern United States, is always pronounced "Nez Purse." Therefore, the accent on the final e of Perce has been omitted in this novel.

Spirit of the Winding Water

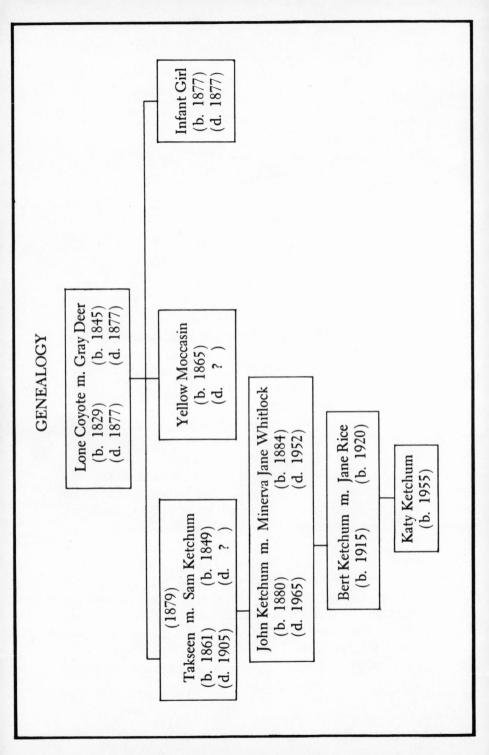

GENEALOGY

Lone Coyote m. Gray Deer
(b. 1829)   (b. 1845)
(d. 1877)   (d. 1877)

Infant Girl
(b. 1877)
(d. 1877)

Yellow Moccasin
(b. 1865)
(d.   ?)

(1879)
Takseen   m.   Sam Ketchum
(b. 1861)   (b. 1849)
(d. 1905)   (d.   ?)

John Ketchum m. Minerva Jane Whitlock
(b. 1880)   (b. 1884)
(d. 1965)   (d. 1952)

Bert Ketchum m. Jane Rice
(b. 1915)   (b. 1920)

Katy Ketchum
(b. 1955)

1

The last thing Katy Ketchum had expected that bright day in April was the shattering of all her plans for the future, hers and Richard's. Her pride in her Indian heritage had been scorned and wedding plans she had cherished since girlhood became merely a lost dream.

She recalled with hurt and anger the words that had changed her vision from a honeymoon pilgrimage to the Bitterroots into a solitary wilderness journey.

"All right, Richard," she had said when he'd broken the news, "you know me well enough to be honest. Did your mother contribute to this decision? What did she say?"

"Oh, just something about your grandmother being an Indian, that you weren't pure . . ."

"Exact words," she'd insisted, refusing to let him soften the sense of the older woman's words.

Richard had sighed. " 'Son,' Mother told me, 'you've got to forget that girl. She's got bad blood in her, and I'll not have black-eyed, red-skinned bastards for grandchildren. I forbid you to see her again.' "

Katy had shut her lips tightly to prevent the indignant

13

protest that was clamoring to be voiced. Her great-grand-mother Takseen, a full-blooded Nez Perce, had always been a source of pride to her, a distant wraith whose spirit some-times seemingly pervaded Katy's spirit in her love for the mountains and the wilderness. She had a strong sense of identity with her heritage, and her lifelong dream had been to trace the link with her Indian past.

The vulgar prejudice expressed by Richard's mother came as a shock. Even more shocking and disappointing was Richard's lack of resistance to his mother's interference. Katy had watched his slump-shouldered departure with utter heaviness, stunned by this weakness in his nature she had never suspected.

The incident was behind her now, that and the ugly en-counter that had followed. What really mattered was the wilderness sojourn she had undertaken, the trip that would renew her joy in life and maybe even satisfy her longing for knowledge of her roots. The mountains had worked their therapeutic magic on her before and she shook off her memo-ries to concentrate on the beauty at hand.

Katy paused and surveyed the side of the mountain, her ears listening for the sound that would identify her trail. Then she smiled with satisfaction as her eyes and ears regis-tered simultaneously the sound and sight of water sliding over rocks. That spring, according to Grandpa John's in-structions of twelve years earlier, was the landmark indicating the trail to old Sam Ketchum's cabin. Panting with the exer-tion of her uphill climb, Katy reached the spring at last and cupped her hands in the icy water that burst from the moun-tainside. The water rushed headlong down the timbered slopes to join Big Creek hundreds of feet below.

Her father's words that had preceded her solitary journey into the wilderness of northern Idaho's Bitterroot Mountains came back to her. "Katy, you can't expect to find Great-grandpa's cabin site with nothing more to guide you than that dusty old journal."

The memory of those remarks, and many others like them, gave her a secret satisfaction, for there it was, the spring Grandpa John had described to her, located above the junction of McBride and Big creeks, with an ever so faint remnant of a trail leading toward the ridge of Moose Meadow Hill. It must have been a peculiarity of early cartographers to call these mountains "hills." So thinking, Katy Ketchum eased the thirty-five-pound pack off her back and propped herself against a tree for a ten-minute rest.

Reaching into a waterproof sidepocket of her pack, she extracted the precious, frayed little red leather journal her grandfather had put in her possession twelve years earlier when she was a child of ten, just before he'd died. Holding it with a reverence born of pride in her Nez Perce heritage, she carefully turned to the note at the back, written in her grandfather's tiny, neat script.

The brief inscription read, "This journal discovered July, 1955, beneath the floorboards of my father's cabin. It is an account written by my father, Sam Ketchum, of the years 1879-1881 when he trapped and mined the streams of Moose Meadow Hill country with his beloved companion, my mother Sarah, a Nez Perce Indian woman, also called by her Indian name Takseen, or Willow."

Katy replaced the volume in her pack after carefully wrapping it in plastic. Then, stooping over the spring, she took a final drink from its waters. With the pack once more in place she proceeded up the faint side trail, her heart pounding more from excitement than exertion. The picture in her mind, formed from Grandpa John's stories to her as a child, made it easy to visualize the cabin site that was her goal. She saw it in her mind, situated at the edge of the timber, just beneath Moose Meadow Ridge, overlooking a broad natural meadow.

The wind changed and Katy smelled an unnatural scent in that remote stretch of wilderness, now national forest land but formerly part of the traditional Nez Perce tribal lands. The odor of loose range stock was unmistakable, and she heard cowbells clanging with the enthusiastic resonance of a call to dinner as the half-wild stock ran pell-mell into the timber at her approach.

She entered the clearing and anxiously scanned the edge of the timber for an indication of the cabin's remains. It was more than twenty years since Grandpa John had revisited the site, discovering only skeletal half-walls left of the dwelling. She hoped those twenty years hadn't destroyed those last vestiges of the cabin. Her initial disappointment at seeing no visible structure was countered by the sight of a boulder a hundred yards away, unnatural in its position, indicating to her the marker she was looking for.

Disregarding her aching shoulders, Katy hastened over the last hundred yards and saw, joyfully, tearfully, the foundation logs that symbolized her beginnings in that land, beginnings that for her went back centuries before the white man had ever set foot on Idaho territory. She knelt reverently before the gray boulder beneath which, she knew, rested the remains of her great-grandmother, Takseen.

As she knelt, she remembered the kindly admonitions of her mother. "My dear daughter," she had chided patiently early that summer, "you simply can't undertake this trip into the wilds alone. Really, I'm not sure I understand your reasons for going."

Just as patiently, Katy had tried to express the significance of the pilgrimage she wished to undertake. Her explanation had not included any reference to Richard, and her mother was too kind to pry.

Instead, she'd told her mother, "I want to trace my roots, Momma. I am *compelled* to know more of my Indian blood. Grandpa taught me to take pride in it. We know so little of great-grandmother, only that she participated in the great trek to Canada with Chief Joseph's band in the Indian War of 1877. We know she led a tragic life, but I want to know more." Grandpa John had hinted at the strong possibility of another journal kept by his father, old Sam Ketchum, but he'd never had the opportunity to return to Moose Meadow Hill to search for it.

So it had been more than a sense of personal urgency that led her to the place where she now knelt. The possibility lay, like a succulent fruit just out of reach, of another journal hidden somewhere nearby, from which she might glean more knowledge of her ancestry.

Katy stood up and surveyed the scattered timbers. "Grandpa, I've kept my promise to you. I've come back to the cabin of your birth just as you wanted," she whispered half-aloud, wishing his spiritual presence were close at hand. Dear Grandpa, half Nez Perce, who had instilled in her the closeness to nature that was the well-spring of strength to her Indian forebears.

With a sense of peace she set up her modest camp, consisting of a poncho rigged for shelter over her down sleeping bag. Then she started a kettle of water to heat over a small fire. To this kettle, Katy added a packet of freeze-dried stew. That meager meal, made complete with the luxury of a cup of hot tea, satisfied her. Her slender, narrow-waisted frame seemed to require little nourishment. Katy's slimness was reflected in her face, with its prominent cheekbones that somehow emphasized her intensely blue, wide-set eyes. Brushing a long, wayward strand of black hair from her eyes, Katy finished the clean-up chores from her simple meal and dropped cross-legged onto her sleeping bag. In spite of good intentions, hurtful conversations intruded themselves into her thoughts, and her muscles tensed to the point that she involuntarily jumped when a figure emerged from the dense stand of pines beyond the campfire. The growing darkness shadowed his face.

"Hello there, Miss. Everything okay here?" his voice broke into the silence. Surprised and a little startled, Katy was relieved to see the uniform of a forest-service ranger as the man approached the fire.

"Good evening," she replied.

"Saw the smoke from your cooking fire and thought I'd investigate. Fire danger's pretty high this summer. Hasn't been a decent rain since Memorial Day."

"I'm sorry, sir." Katy stood up. "Can I get a fire permit from you?"

"The name's Matthew Moss," the tall young man said, indicating the name plate on his uniform. "My friends call me Matt. I can issue you one right here, but you must use extra precaution until we get some rain."

Matthew propped a knee on a stump and rested a pad of paper on it. He proceeded to write up the slip, inquiring as to her name, proposed length of stay, and approximate whereabouts during that time.

While he wrote, Katy studied him. The short pencil stub was nearly lost in his large hand and a slight awkwardness in his writing suggested to Katy that he'd prefer cruising timber or hiking the high country to filling out government forms. She liked his open, honest face and his solid appearance.

Matt looked up. His curiosity got the best of him, and his good-natured smile won Katy's confidence.

"Do you mind if I ask an obvious question?" he inquired, handing her the fire permit.

"You're wondering what I'm doing all alone up here on top of a mountain, right?" Katy replied. "Would you like some tea, by the way?"

"Wouldn't mind a bit. Thanks." He watched her silently as she shared her tea bag and a packet of sugar, filling her spare tin cup with the hot brew. The silence lay between them while he awaited her response, not prying, just waiting.

Katy sat down again. "I was searching for this particular cabin site. From the stories I heard as a child I was able to locate this spot where my great-grandparents lived. Great-grandpa was a trapper, but he did a little mining too, around 1880."

Matt's interest was aroused. "You mean you know for a fact that this was his cabin?" He looked over at the cabin ruins. The sill logs were still solidly in place, ax-cut ends protruding from corners where the lower logs still rested in their notches.

"I do indeed. My great-grandmother is buried beneath that boulder over there. She was a full-blooded Nez Perce woman. Great-grandpa called her Sarah, but her Indian name was Takseen, which translates as 'Willow.' "

Matt's eyes lit up with interest. "No kidding. I can see why you were interested in coming here. Sort of a pilgrimage, I'd guess."

"You really understand, don't you?" Katy said softly, impressed by his intuition. "There's not one in a hundred who know or could begin to understand my innermost feelings about this place. You see, I'm very proud of my Indian blood. Sarah participated in the great trek with Chief Joseph and his people to avoid being put on the reservation at Lapwai. From what little I know, she suffered terribly during the journey to Canada. The young warrior she was to marry was killed in the Big Hole Massacre along with most of her family. She was apparently without anyone, possibly only a brother, at the time of the surrender, yet she somehow escaped to Canada with some of White Bird's people. She later made her way back to Idaho and met and married a white trapper, Sam Ketchum."

Matt whistled softly. "That's an intriguing story, almost gives me the shivers. There's much more you'd like to know, right?" He rested his chin on his hand and shook his head sadly. "Our treatment of the Nez Perce during that campaign was a shabby thing. I've done a lot of reading about it. In fact, I've retraced several portions of their fourteen-hundred-mile escape route, including most of the battle and skirmish sites along the way. It's a powerful and tragic chapter in the history of the American Indian." He looked up with an embarrassed smile. "I didn't mean to sound stuffy."

Katy's smile encouraged him to go on. "It's just that the subject is kind of dear to my heart. I've spent my whole life in this neck of the woods, and I can truly identify with those people and the strong feeling they had for their tribal lands."

It had grown dark and Katy added some branches to the fire. "I'm really amazed. We seem to share the same sentiments." She added bitterly, almost under her breath, "I wish Richard understood a tenth as well what I'm doing and why."

"Richard?"

"Richard was my fiancé."

The silence that followed gave Katy a chance to decide how far to go in sharing confidences with a complete stranger. He didn't intrude into her silence, and she decided to tell him.

"I don't want to waste your time with my problems, Matt, but would you believe," she continued as she pulled a wrinkled letter from her pocket, "would you believe," she repeated emphatically, "that Richard's parents are ashamed for him to be engaged to a girl who is one-eighth Indian?"

She smoothed the letter on her knee and Matt could see that she was upset.

"Richard has decided it would be best for us not to see each other for the rest of the summer. Richard's mother has decided it would be best for us not to see each other for the rest of our lives. Mind you, he says he's not ashamed of my background, but he wants to make a compromise to respect his parents' feelings, so we're not seeing each other for three months. I'm pretty shocked about the whole thing. I never had any indication of such feelings on the part of his family before this summer." She lifted her chin stubbornly. "I feel like telling him to go to hell, but darn it all, I still love him."

Katy pulled her jacket around her shoulders and shivered. "I'm not in the habit of making such outbursts to strangers. I'm really sorry."

"Don't think a thing of it. You said you were planning to be here for a week. You'll have a chance to do some good hard thinking, and in the meantime, maybe you'll find something around here to add to your knowledge of the past. What are you hoping to find, by the way?"

Katy appreciated his changing the subject. "I'll show you the journal my grandfather, who was born right here, discovered a little more than twenty years ago. He found it in a dynamite box under the floorboards of the cabin. He remembered his father keeping the journal and was sure of its existence, so he came back and looked until he found it."

Matt turned the stained pages thoughtfully, holding the journal close to the fire in order to see the cramped writing.

"Anyway, there's some indication there might have been a second volume. Just before his mother died, Grandpa thinks his father wrote down a lot of the information he had gleaned from Sarah about her early life and of her experiences in the Nez Perce Indian War. Her recollections were for the most part sad ones, and she wasn't given to talking about them freely. What I'm hoping is that old Sam Ketchum may have compiled the things she'd told him into a second volume. I'm going to do some prowling around on that possibility."

"Well, I wish you luck," Matt said rising. He extended his hand to her. "You're a spunky girl, and I think you'll get what you go after. I've got to get back to the tower. It's about a two-mile hike from here. I'm only up there temporarily while the fire danger's high."

"Thanks for dropping by. I guess I needed someone to talk to."

"I enjoyed it. Your ancestors picked a pretty spot to settle. In fact, I come here often myself. You may have noticed the well-worn trail behind the cabin."

"No, I didn't, but I'll bet you're responsible for the fire-pit and that comfy stump!"

"You guessed it! Take it easy and don't worry about a thing. You're perfectly safe here, but watch out for fires. There's been a lot of heat lightning on these warm nights."

Katy watched the broad-shouldered figure until he was out of sight, then unrolled her sleeping bag. Within minutes she fell into a troubled sleep.

2

Katy's restlessness became discomfort as she tossed within the confining sleeping bag. Its nylon outer layer made it slippery, and soon it was twisted under her in a way that made sleep impossible. She crawled out and straightened the bag, then tried again, this time tucking her red down vest beneath her head for a pillow. Sleep still wouldn't come as she pondered the disturbing contemts of Richard's letter.

His parents were well-to-do, owning a large potato-processing plant in southern Idaho. She was unwilling to admit that Richard would succumb to the will of his dominating mother. Still, his parents were good people, active in the community and the church, and had given their only child a great deal of love.

Richard, a third-year law student at the University of Idaho, was spending the summer assisting the prosecuting attorney in Blackfoot County.

She pounded her fist ineffectually against the softness of her sleeping bag but took no comfort from its smooth warmth. How could their relationship deteriorate so after the passionate intensity they had shared for more than a year? Katy had been devoted to Richard, and he had seemed to reciprocate the feeling in every respect. They had met when she was a senior and he a second-year law student. They were immediately attracted by their common interests, especially their love for the mountains. They'd shared so many interesting times. She smiled as she remembered the trips to the ghost towns in the northern part of the state, how they'd talked to the old-timers who remembered stories of the boom times of the gold-rush days. They'd bicycled through many miles of beautiful countryside together, and they'd shared the quiet intimacy of studying companionably for the never-ending rounds of exams. Trouble hadn't started until she'd been a guest in his home during Easter break earlier that spring.

"I must shake off this nonsense," she determined, and firmly put the dilemma out of her mind. She turned her thoughts to pleasanter things, particularly the possibility of finding another journal. Fitful sleep came at last and with it, a disturbing dream.

"Katy, Takseen," an unseen voice was whispering from nowhere and everywhere. "Follow me," the voice urged. A path led down to a willow-covered bank beside a small clear stream. Perched in an overhanging willow branch was a small brown owl. Its eyes held hers in an unblinking stare across the water. Its beak was unmoving, yet a voice issued in a whisper from it.

"I am Soklahtomah, the *wyakin* of Takseen." The thoughts issued without visible movement, registering with clarity on Katy's brain, as she was given to understand that this owl was the special attending spirit, or *wyakin*, of Takseen. The image of a young Indian girl materialized before her, dressed in a white-fringed doeskin dress with intricate beading and quillwork decorating the front of it. Her legs and feet were encased in soft leather leggings and moccasins and her heavy dark braids framed a handsome face. She gestured for Katy to follow, her mournful black eyes compelling her forward. Katy's feet seemingly floated over the sage and underbrush as the trail took a steep turn up a ravine. Then the Indian girl paused, pointing beneath a large pine tree where lay the scattered bones of a corpse. On the skull there remained a token patch of long black hair beside a naked spot indicating that its owner had doubtless been scalped. Katy's attention was attracted by a fluttering overhead as the solemn owl lighted on a branch, fixing her gaze again with its hypnotic stare.

"Here lies Buffalo Robe, noble warrior of the Nez Perce. His corpse was mutilated and his burial place desecrated one hundred years ago by Bannock scouts," the thoughts registered in her brain again. A sudden snarl chilled her, and, glancing into the dense sage, Katy glimpsed a coyote slinking by. It paused and curled its lips in a painful grimace, then disappeared.

"A restless spirit," the owl continued, indicating the spot where the coyote had disappeared, "doomed to wander forever until these bones receive proper burial."

The vision of the lovely Indian girl merged with that of the owl and grew larger and larger in her sight until Katy's whole being was encompassed by it. The final message resounded in her ears. "You will know more of this. You will find this place, daughter of the people, and restore these blessed bones. I will guide you in your mission." There was a whirr of wings, then only blackness and silence.

Katy awoke in a cold sweat. Her hands felt her face and head as if to assure herself that they were unchanged. Her head felt swollen, almost to exploding, and very, very heavy. The descending notes of a screech owl riveted her attention, bringing vividly to mind her dream. Was it a dream or a vision, she thought incredulously as she listened to the notes of the owl. Gathering courage, she answered its wavering call, causing it to approach ever nearer until it settled on a branch close by and hooted the last questioning notes of its call. Then it was gone.

Katy drew the edges of the nylon bag about her ears, shivering as she recalled each detail of the dream. Finally a sense of peace descended upon her. "So be it," she thought. "If the guardian spirits of my ancestors are guiding me, I will accept their presence." At last she fell into a deep and untroubled sleep, not even interrupted by the first rays of the sun that spread their welcome warmth across the upland meadow. She dozed on until the sun was an hour above the horizon, then rose to prepare a cup of hot chocolate, meanwhile changing to a clean pair of cut-offs and a red and white striped T-shirt.

Perched on Matthew's pine stump, Katy drank in the beauty of the meadow. There was no intrusive odor of cattle that morning, only the brisk freshness of the mountain air. High overhead she heard the stirrings as of an approaching locomotive as the wind sighed through the ridge of lodgepole pines behind her, rising in intensity, then slowly falling away in a repetitious wavelike pattern. The meadow was carpeted with the vivid reds and blues and yellows of Indian paintbrush, lupine, and butterweed.

Katy felt refreshed, yet noted a sense of disquiet, something unfulfilled tugging at her subconscious. Her strange dream of the previous night returned to her once again. The dream's supernatural quality persisted, even though she tried to analyze it in a logical fashion.

"I don't believe in spirit possession," she affirmed to herself. Yet there had been an overwhelming heaviness in her head as the vision of the owl and the Indian girl had merged and encompassed her whole body. It had felt as if another conscious mind were superimposing itself upon her own.

"Why the coincidence of the screech owl's presence immediately after my dream?" she wondered further. The answer, Katy insisted to herself, was simply that the penetrating call of the owl had occurred *before* her dream, causing her to dream of the owl, just as a telephone ringing can cause a sleeper to incorporate that sound into his dream.

Having thus disposed of the lingering, disturbing sensation following her dream, Katy turned her attention to the cabin site.

The foundation was more or less intact, though it provided a precarious footing, for many of the floorboards were rotten and a few were missing. The north and east walls were represented by a row of three or four weathered logs, most of the logs of the other walls being scattered in the grass adjacent to the cabin.

A few yards east of the cabin was the rock that was Sarah's burial marker. Katy's attention was drawn by it. This marker seemed a logical place to begin her search. She examined it closely for any inscription, but found none. It seemed the right thing, somehow, to pause before it in meditation, and Katy inwardly sought guidance from a source greater than herself. She could willingly believe, as her forebears had, in the spiritual existence of all life around her, even in attending spirits. Such belief was closely tied to her strong identification with all of nature, and in her mind there was nothing unchristian about such a philosophy.

She spent the balance of the morning puttering around the cabin, trying to remove loose floorboards, but succeeded in unearthing nothing more than a nest of field mice ensconced beneath the sill log.

At noon, Katy nibbled on some crackers and sandwich spread and finished up with a handful of hard candies and a fruit drink. Her morning's efforts had been unsuccessful and she decided to spend part of the afternoon exploring the ridge above her.

A hundred vertical feet of climbing took her to the summit of the ridge. The view from it offered a glimpse of rounded, timber-covered slopes as mountains rolled away in every direction. Dense stands of lodgepole pine covered Moose Meadow Ridge. It was clean timber and the underbrush was minimal. Katy saw, to her delight, browsing on the grassy carpet, a young doe and her half-grown fawn. A shaft of afternoon sunlight caught the pair, but as Katy watched, the light suddenly vanished. Looking up, she realized a whole cloud bank had rolled in without her notice. "Matt will be pleased," she thought to herself. "A good soaker should eliminate the fire danger."

With all the suddenness that only a mountain storm can exhibit, the first fat drops were upon her and Katy made her way down the steep slope. The going was easy, however, because of the lack of undergrowth, and she arrived, sopping wet, but exhilarated, at her camp.

She wrapped herself in her orange poncho. Hoping the nylon stuff bag containing her sleeping bag was indeed waterproof, she covered it, along with a pile of hastily gathered equipment, with her ground tarp. "I should have known better than to leave camp unprepared for something like this," she chided herself.

She sat out the rain, huddled inside the poncho and shivered a little, deriving what measure of protection she could from the overhanging tree branches.

The rain lasted no more than an hour, and once the sun was out, her equipment soon dried. Having a sense of complete privacy, Katy gave no thought to changing her wet clothing with only the shelter of a tree, so that she was considerably startled to hear a voice, just as she pulled a dry yellow T-shirt down over her head.

"Excuse me ma'am, I didn't mean to frighten you." It was Matthew Moss again, to both her relief and her embarrassment. Katy turned toward him, not sure how long he had been standing there, but the embarrassment was evident in her face, she was certain.

"I just got here," he said, reading her mind, though a faint redness showed against his tan cheeks. "Didn't mean to, uh, startle you. Just thought I'd check up on you before I leave the hill."

"You're not staying at the tower any longer?" Katy inquired, regaining a little of her composure.

"No, the fire danger's nothing to worry about after this rain, and the fellows at Big Creek station will be needing me back there. We're a little short-handed this summer, and I've got my hands full with timber sales and that clearcutting mess on Squaw Peak." Matt sat down on a stump with a sigh. "To tell you the truth, I much prefer the solitude of the tower to all the paperwork at the ranger station. I never thought forest service work would keep me at a desk so much of the time!"

"I can understand how you feel," she sympathized.

"Anything new in your search?" Matt inquired as she seated herself on her now dry poncho.

"I'm afraid I didn't accomplish much today," she admitted. Something in his understanding nature communicated itself to Katy, and she again felt the impulse to confide in him.

"Would you mind listening to a dream I had last night? It probably has no significance, yet it was so vivid that I can't quite get it out of my mind."

"Why sure," he encouraged her, "let's hear it. I don't have to be on my way for at least a half hour."

Katy told him the details of her strange dream, including the sense of heaviness she had experienced upon awakening and the coincidental calling of the screech owl.

Matt pondered her description for a moment. Then he looked at her sharply. "Do you believe in reincarnation?"

Katy was startled. "Are you kidding?"

"No. Seriously."

"I didn't mean to be rude. I guess there's a lot of support for that theory, but personally, I've never accepted it—probably because I don't like what it does to the idea of having a family. When my first baby is born," she explained, idly toying with a blade of grass, "I don't want to think some spirit chose my baby as a vehicle to work out the sins of its past lives."

"I know what you mean," Matt agreed, "but I've given it a lot of serious thought, and I haven't ruled out its possibility. Suppose there was such a thing." He smiled self-consciously, and Katy didn't know if he was joking as he continued. "Suppose you are a reincarnation of your Indian great-grandmother, Takseen. From the tragic life you've indicated that she led, she could be seeking, through you, to make amends for what happened."

"You better elaborate on that," Katy said, not persuaded.

Matt stood up, caught up now in the story he was weaving. "Well, first of all, you said that the voice calling you in your dream said, 'Katy, Takseen,' as if you were one and the same."

"I hadn't thought of that."

"And second, the little owl indicated that you had a task to perform, a mission, to settle the wandering spirit of Buffalo Robe, that is, to find his grave and give his bones a decent burial."

"Surely you can't believe all this," Katy shook her head wonderingly.

"I know it sounds strange, and no, I don't necessarily believe it, but you asked for an interpretation of your dream. Carrying it even farther—or don't you want me to?" he asked, embarrassed at his own eagerness.

"Go ahead," she encouraged him softly with a puzzled look on her face. She thought privately that his boyish enthusiasm was a good quality, and she didn't want to appear to humor him.

"This will really sound farfetched to you, but it is entirely possible, accepting the idea of reincarnation of course——"

"Which is admittedly a big step," she interrupted.

"Right. Then assuming the possibility of reincarnation," Matt continued, "Richard could be a reincarnation of Buffalo Robe, and, because their relationship was unfulfilled a hundred years ago, Takseen and Buffalo Robe are seeking fulfillment in this life."

"Then why is Richard putting me off?" she inquired a little dully, unpleasantly brought back to her problem.

"I'm not sure I can answer that." Matt sat down again, embarrassed, regretting a little having let his imagination get away with him. Katy noted for a second time a shade of red beneath the tan of his face. Something indefinable tugged at her mind, but she put it aside.

"Believe me, if I knew where the bones of Buffalo Robe lay, I would restore them. I would do it willingly for the memory of Buffalo Robe and Takseen. However, I really doubt that Richard and his family would find the restoration of an Indian's grave sufficient reason to overcome a long-standing prejudice, or that our former relationship would be restored."

Katy shook her head sadly and stood up. "Thank you for your interpretation. I'm afraid I'm not convinced, yet in some ways, your version is rather remarkable and quite beautiful. I would like to believe it, in fact. Perhaps the *wyakin* of Takseen would guide me to the gravesite or even to the missing journal and give me insight into those dim and tragic events of a hundred years ago. Though I reject reincarnation, I feel a strong spiritual presence in this spot, as I do in all of nature."

"Those are beautiful thoughts," Matt agreed softly.

"Please don't think I was making light of your reasons for
being here. I truly admire what you're doing." He walked
over to her, extending his hand. "I've got to be going now.
Perhaps we'll meet again." Her hand was warm in his
larger one and she left it there longer than necessary, acutely
aware of a rush of loneliness in this wilderness setting. "Maybe we've known one another in a former life," he teased. "I
feel as though we share many common bonds." He gave her
hand a final squeeze. "I'll be seeing you, and good luck.
Why don't you check in at the Big Creek Ranger Station
before you leave the area and let me know how things have
been going?"

"It's a promise," she said, her large blue eyes meeting
his warm brown ones. They shared a friendly smile, and he
was gone.

3

"Takseen, open your eyes." It was the voice again, intruding into her sleep. She let herself be caught up in the haunting whisper, and did as it commanded. "Up here, look." It was a warm moonlit night, and she saw above her, bathed in a silver glow, the figure of the little brown screech owl.

Katy remained in a trance-like state, neither sleeping nor waking as she looked intently at the owl, eerie in the silver light, yet somehow not the least bit terrifying.

"I am Soklahtomah, your friend. Do not be afraid." It stretched its wings as it perched on the branch. "I'm here to help you. The dwelling place to which I fly will reveal its secrets. Watch closely. I cannot come to you again."

There was a soft whirring of wings as it took flight, brushing past her shoulder, alighting in a dead tree ten yards from the cabin. The gray trunk no longer stood upright, but was supported at a precarious angle by its neighbor, a tall, upright pine.

As she watched, Katy heard again the haunting, descending notes of the screech owl. This time it was answered by a mate a little distance away. The calls continued back and forth, the mate approaching closer with each response until it joined the first owl on the dead tree, and together they disappeared into a hole in the trunk about eight feet above the ground.

The gray trunk was turned to silver in the reflected beauty of the moon, and only the scampering, furtive sounds of the night creatures were to be heard. From the tree there was silence.

Katy awoke with no memory of the previous night. Her camp activities had by then fallen into a routine, and she performed them effortlessly. She spent the morning repeating her search of the cabin foundation. Again her efforts were unrewarded.

It was late afternoon when she mixed a cup of fruit drink, and, with a handful of nuts and hard candies, took the journal and her mattress pad a little way beyond the cabin for a brief snack and a rest.

Propped up against a tree on her compact foam pad, she thought, with sheer pleasure, "What luxury." The solitary wilderness experience indeed seemed a panacea for all her problems, even if only temporarily. Katy sipped her drink, studying the journal closely, though she'd read it over and over many times, hoping anew for a bit of information that might guide her search.

Her attention was diverted by a bird song that she couldn't identify. Trying to spot the singer of the clear, warbling notes, she scanned the trees behind the cabin.

With a start of recognition, she saw a bare gray trunk leaning against a neighboring pine, and a memory teased at the edges of her mind. "Something I dreamed?" she mused as the image darted about within her brain, coming forward to the conscious level, only to retreat again. Then she saw a small hole in the tree, appearing like a dark smudge from that distance, and her memory was awakened.

"Dear God," she whispered. "The owl. That nest." Chills ran up her spine and raised the hair on the back of her neck as she set the journal aside and walked swiftly to the decaying tree. Her mind raced frantically in expectation, not daring to accept the dream of the night before. Could it have been a prophetic dream? Had she actually risen from her bed to follow that creature to its nest? She was perplexed and excited, unable to answer her own questions.

There was indeed a hollow nest and Katy stood on tiptoe, eagerly thrusting her hand upward, knowing only too well she lacked a good six inches of reaching it. She hastily dragged a broken floorboard over, setting it on edge against the tree and balancing precariously on it. That time her hand gained access to the hole and plunged recklessly in. "Serve me right to get nipped by its occupant," she thought. But there was no furry or feathery occupant; rather, a metallic hardness met her groping fingers.

"A box!" she cried aloud, tugging at it, urging it through the opening, which was barely large enough to contain it.

It was indeed a box, but to Katy's disappointment, the lid was rusted shut and resisted all efforts to pry it open.

Carrying the box carefully back to camp, Katy couldn't resist a gentle shake. Something slid back and forth and there was a rolling noise that she could not identify.

Excited, Katy scraped at the edges of the lid with her pocketknife, scratching away some of the rust, finally inserting the edge of a blade into the crack. It resisted, but she persisted until finally the lid gave way.

Katy offered a silent prayer of thanks when she saw the treasure that lay within. There was a little red leather volume, very much like the other, and as she lifted it tenderly from the box, she saw that the writing on the yellowed pages was indeed the same small, neat script of Sam Ketchum, reminding her of Grandpa John's handwriting.

Her heart dropped, however, when she saw that moisture had attacked the edges of some of the pages, making portions of the manuscript illegible.

As she scanned the pages, Katy saw the names "Big Hole," "White Bird," "Bear Paws," and a number of others that indicated that surely this contained an account of Takseen's experiences in the Nez Perce War, just as she had hoped.

There was yet another treasure within the box, and Katy put away the volume to examine it. A lovely little moss agate hung on a leather thong. She examined the dendritic pattern of the stone more closely and was surprised to see that it closely resembled a bird. In fact, the resemblance to an owl was unmistakable, and Katy blinked her eyes to make certain she wasn't imagining things.

She slipped the leather thong over her head, letting the cool stone rest inside her shirt against her skin. Then she collected her belongings from the resting spot she had abandoned, carrying the two journals carefully back to camp.

Katy spent at least thirty minutes laying in a good supply of wood. She was determined to have sufficient firelight to read by, in order to complete the entire journal that evening.

She gave no thought to supper; her excitement at the thrilling discovery gave no room for satisfying the hunger that went unnoticed.

She performed all the routine chores necessary for the evening so that she would have a completely uninterrupted period for reading. The anticipation was more than she could bear, so with an hour of daylight still left, she began her perusal of the volume.

Katy gasped with surprise and affection as she read her great-grandfather's introduction, surprised at its content, which provided information previously unknown, and touched by his intense devotion to the Indian girl, Takseen.

The writing was small and neat, the edges of the beginning pages undamaged by moisture, so Katy had no difficulty in aborbing its contents. She was already familiar with Sam Ketchum's unlettered but straightforward style.

October, 1905

In these pages I hope to tell how I, Sam Ketchum, an old fellow who's bettered himself no more than to make a living trapping and mining, but who's done no worse than a smidgin' of whiskey trading, came to marry the best goldurn Injun Squaw a man could ask for. But mostly, this is her story, her recollections, as well as I can remember, of the things she told me about her life with the Injuns. She was born Takseen, a Nez Perce word meaning Willow, but I called her Sarah after my Mother back in Ohio. God rest Her soul. Sarah had an unhappy life with the Nez Perce, having the misfortune to be born a Wallamwatkin under Chief Joseph at the time the White men were giving them Hell. She traveled with Joseph and his people for fourteen hundred miles to avoid the one-armed soldier chief's* order to go to the reservation at Lapwai. I'll write more later about how she escaped to Canada while most of the survivors of Joseph's people were forced to surrender at the Bear Paw's.

But first let me say that I am writing this because I love Sarah, and my heart is breaking because she is dying of a fever and only God can ease her Suffering now. She was never one to talk much of her early life because it was so sad—losing every Soul she ever loved—her family and the Warrior she was betrothed to, and I know she wouldn't want me blabbering her story around, because she has so much Pride. But nonetheless, I will tell her

---

*General O. O. Howard.

story, and I will probably have to hide these pages or she will sure to God make me tear them up if she finds out.

John, our only living child, is now full-grown, having married a young Lady by the name of Minerva Whitlock, and is working in Spokane. He may never see these pages, but if he does, I want him to know he can take Pride in being a half-breed, for there is no finer Injuns than the Nez Perce, and his mother is among the finest of her People. I say this with all my heart.

Katy was genuinely touched by the intense feelings set forth by her great-grandfather, and she read on with blurred vision.

I will quit my ramblings and write the story as it is now written in my heart, and though no one may ever read these pages, it would do the world good to see the miserable way in which Man treated his fellow Man in the Nez Perce Injun War of 1877. By that I mean how the White man treated the Injuns whose only sin was to own the prettiest piece of grazing land in the most beautiful valley God ever made. The Injuns knew it as the Wallowa Valley, the Valley of the Winding Water. The White settlers were jealous of the fine horses and cattle the Injuns bred, and of course, when the greatest Evil of all, Gold, was discovered in this same area, the White man had to move the Injuns off their tribal lands to satisfy their Greed.

Takseen (I will call her by her Injun name since this is her story) was born about 1861, judging by the fact that she later knew there was a great War being waged between the White men about the time of her birth. She was a young girl of fifteen or sixteen when the first real trouble came to the Wallowa Valley. Up until this time there had been several Treaties with the Nez Perce. One Treaty would allow them to keep the Valley, the next would take it away. But the Lower Nez Perce, to which Joseph's band of Wallamwatkins belonged, never agreed to give away the lands in which the bones of their Fathers were buried. Still, they patiently suffered at the hands of settlers and miners who used Treachery and all manner of Evil—horse-stealing, whiskey-selling, and outright Murder —to heat up the blood of the young men and cause trouble so that the whole Tribe would get in trouble and be sent to the Reservation at Lapwai where some of the Upper Nez Perce had already gone.

Takseen remembers only a few years of real peace as a young girl and of course her memory is stronger (and therefore all the sadder) because she was at this time in love with a young Warrior by the name of Buffalo Robe. He was, by all accounts, a fine and handsome young man, who showed much Bravery upon the field of Battle, but lost his life soon after at the infamous Big Hole Massacre before the two had ever become Husband and Wife.

One time I made Takseen tell me how the Injuns of her day courted, and she, Blushing all the while, told me this story of her and Buffalo Robe. She first met him at a creek called the Place of the Swallows, and because he was Enamored of her, he began to spend his evenings serenading her with a flageolet, in the manner of young men who court an Injun Maiden. She, in turn . . .

Katy turned the page, only to discover, to her dismay, that the margins of the following pages were stained, blotting out fragments of the story, making it nearly impossible to read. Nightfall was upon her, and in the flickering firelight she had difficulty making sense of the yellowed, stained pages.

Sighing with disappointment Katy had no choice but to

retire and wait for daylight to try to decipher the intriguing story. It worked upon her imagination, both the beginning pages and those as yet unread, and her dreams vividly incorporated the figures of Takseen and Buffalo Robe into the lovely setting of the Wallowa Valley, the Valley of the Winding Water.

It was a sultry morning, with another rainstorm in the offing. Katy had wrapped her gear to protect it and had hiked to the top of the ridge to a rock ledge she had spotted the first day. Not only was the view superb from that vantage point, but the ledge offered shelter in the event of a storm.

It was still early morning when Katy settled herself atop the rocky outcrop. She had brought her poncho along in the event of rain and, for good measure, had brought the tin box to protect the journals. The ledge that would give shelter as soon as the storm arrived, as it surely would, was just beneath her.

Katy took a moment to savor the beauty of the mountains around her. The closest ones were gently rounded, reaching only about five thousand feet in elevation, their pine-covered slopes a solid carpet of green. In the distance, where the green became a deep blue, were the higher, rocky peaks, their summits sharp and bare of vegetation, as they stood like rigid sentinels, guarding the vast and trackless wilderness of the Primitive Area.

The sultry air held a threat, and the deepening gray of the sky confirmed that threat. In the west the first sharply etched bolts of lightning were splashing the sky.

They were still distant, however, and because of the proximity of trees on the higher ridge behind her, Katy felt no danger in her vantage point. There would be plenty of opportunity to seek shelter before the storm arrived.

She lifted the moss agate with its owl-like pattern from

beneath her shirt and gazed at it fondly. Surely that amulet had been the property of Takseen. How appropriate was its image of the little owl. It had been an owl that had led Katy to the discovery of the journal. Whether its presence had been physical or spiritual or imaginary, she was unable to answer. The owl had nevertheless been responsible for her finding the journal with its precious contents.

She replaced the stone, enjoying the physical contact with a possession of her great-grandmother's, feeling closer to the story to which she now turned her attention. The cool stone, warmed by her flesh, seemingly penetrated to her heart with its warmth, enveloping her in an almost spiritual presence.

Katy had brought a notebook along, and carefully transcribed the contents of the stained pages as she deciphered them and put the story together. It took nearly an hour to put together the pieces of the courtship of Takseen and Buffalo Robe. The tale, with missing words tentatively supplied by her, continued. . . .

She, in turn, with the Modesty of a Nez Perce Maiden, let him court her, but gave him no Encouragement. Takseen said that young girls did not talk much with Warriors. Buffalo Robe had the choice of buying her with horses, or Wooing her himself, in hopes of gaining the go-ahead from her and her parents. Young Buffalo Robe, a fine man of good Standing in his band, won the consent of old Lone Coyote, her father, and his young wife, Gray Deer, to marry Takseen. It was early spring of the year 1877, a Fateful year for the Nez Perce. Before a date for the Wedding feast could be agreed upon, the first big Trouble with the White man came. The Treaties entered into up until this time were never signed by the Lower Nez Perce, but the White Fathers agreed that the year

1877 was the year the remaining bands of the Lower Nez Perce should exchange their million acres of grazing lands for a handful of farm plots on the Clearwater reserve at Lapwai. I don't know what went on at all the Councils, but it was clear that there was disagreement between the chiefs. Old Toohoohoolzote was in favor of war, but the Ultimatum issued by General Howard and Agent Monteith gave the Injuns only thirty days to come peaceably to the Reservation or face war. Joseph, Looking Glass, White Bird, and Hush-hush-cute felt like they had no choice. They were Honorable and Peaceable men, and wanted to avoid shedding the Blood of their People.

Their People, though, according to Takseen, were Dismayed at having only thirty days to gather the stock off the high winter range. They could see no way to safely cross the raging Snake that lay between them and Lapwai. It was a Hellish torrent each spring, and many Lives would be lost if they were foolhardy enough to cross in May or June. It was with heavy hearts that the people gathered their scattered stock from the Wallamwatkin ancestral home, the Wallowa Valley. In their hearts, they knew Joseph was right when he said, 'We were like sheep. They were like grizzly bears. . . . If I should fight the whites I would lose all. No man in the world would take all his property and burn it in a fire. So it is with me."

Katy was so absorbed in her transcription that the sound of an approaching wind went unnoticed until the treetops around her suddenly bent double, only to be lashed to and fro by the murderous winds that followed. There were no preliminaries, only a wild blending of sound and fury as the wind and rain bore down upon her, loud claps of thunder resounding through the hills.

Katy's first thought was for the journals, which she immediately put into the tin box. Then, protecting the precious box beneath her poncho, she slid down the rain-slickened rocks of the outcrop. A gust of wind tore her notebook from her grasp and sent it flying. She gained the shelter of the ledge, thrusting the box as far into its depths as possible, then peered toward the trees for a glimpse of her notebook. It was lying ten yards away, wedged against a boulder, and she struggled across the slippery rock slope to retrieve it.

She was never to cover the entire distance. A hideous crack of lightning seared a pine tree atop the ledge, sending it plummeting to earth. Katy, looking up, saw the top of the tree dropping, almost in slow motion. Her only chance was to run straight ahead, up the incline. In her panic, she slipped on a loose rock, twisting her ankle, falling to the ground as the tree simultaneously landed with crushing force on the rocky slope. She lay beneath its limbs, a twisted speck of orange beneath the branches of the pine.

There was no one to witness her unconsciousness, nor were there any witnesses to the frantic flutterings of a small brown owl who flew anxiously over the scene of her toppled nest.

4

The Wallowa Valley—1877

"The young men talk of leaving the valley. Doesn't it make your heart sick?" Takseen questioned her friend Pale Moon as the two young girls plunged their digging sticks into the rich, moist earth. They were working their way along the brow of a steep hill, harvesting the first of the camas roots with the other women and girls.

"We won't be forced to give up our homes," the plain, round-faced girl asserted. "This valley," her hand swept the green valley, encircled by hills, "has been our home long before the *shoyapee*, the white man, set foot on it."

"Yet the young men say, even Joseph says, that we must obey the one-armed soldier chief's order to move to the reservation at Lapwai," answered Takseen, slender as the willow for which she was named, and pretty, with flashing black eyes and waist-length braids.

"This girl will never leave the Wallowa Valley," Pale Moon affirmed with determination and bent her strong young back to the task of harvesting the sweet, tuberous roots.

Takseen's basket was nearly full, and she paused to

45

survey the valley that both of them loved dearly. Beyond the ring of hills thrust the jagged ridges of the lofty Wallowa Mountains. Snow fields glistened in the distance, while all around them the signs of spring were bursting from the earth. Streams from nearby mountains cascaded down the slopes, gathering strength and volume, only to meander sedately but bank-full through the broad green valley with its colorful carpet of flowers.

The heart of Takseen swelled at the beauty around her, and she whispered a brief prayer to Hunyewat, the Deity. "Let this not be my people's last spring in our beloved valley," she prayed.

The girls worked on in silence, weighing their heavy thoughts. Suddenly Pale Moon brightened, saying slyly, "I thought I heard the music of a flageolet near your tepee last night."

"You must have heard the wind sighing through the trees," the slender one evaded.

"If I ask you three times, you must tell the truth," Pale Moon pursued.

"Well, then, perhaps you did hear the courting music of a young man."

"Buffalo Robe?"

Takseen nodded shyly in embarrassment.

"My heart is filled with envy, my friend. He is a fine young man, and very handsome."

"He hasn't yet approached my parents. I have spoken to him only once, at Laaps creek, the Place of the Swallows," Takseen confided. "If he speaks to them concerning marriage, I am sure he'll gain their consent."

"And yours?"

"You must know the answer to that."

Pale Moon seemed pleased that Takseen had made the startling revelation so openly.

The girls lifted the cylindrical pack baskets with their succulent burden and carried them back to camp, where the tepees of Joseph's wealthy band of Wallamwatkins stood beside the banks of a swollen stream. For the rest of the day the girls joined the women in cleaning the camas roots. The harvest was inferior to those that would follow in summer and fall, but there was a sense of urgency in laying up quantities of the staple should that indeed be the last spring in the Wallowa Valley.

It was nearly dark when Yellow Moccasin, the brother of Takseen, rode into camp on his fat little pony, Rabbit Ears. The twelve-year-old boy was puffed up with self-importance from his success at helping the other boys, many of them older than he, round up the loose stock and large pony herds that had been wintering in the nearby valleys.

Takseen could see the good-sized herd straggling in to join the others under the watchful eyes of the herd attendants.

"You've done a man's work today, little brother," she rewarded him with praise.

"Rabbit Ears deserves the credit," the boy protested modestly, but his heart swelled at the comparison to a man.

Yellow Moccasin had long been a worshipful admirer of the warrior Buffalo Robe, longing for the day when he could accompany Buffalo Robe and the other young men across the mountains to the place of the buffalo. He filled his idle hours with fantasies of himself, seated astride a nobler mount than the faithful little Rabbit Ears, slaying the shaggy brown beasts across the shining mountains and winning the acclaim of the adult members of the band.

"I saw a disturbing thing today, my sister," he confided in exchange for the compliment she had paid him. "The white soldiers have come, just as General Howard said they would."

"But they can't occupy our valley. We won't go to war

with the whites," his sister protested. The peaceable philosophy of their respected leader Heinmot Tooyalaket, Chief Joseph, was deeply ingrained in her. It was said by those who remembered such things that in seventy years of acquaintance with the *shoyapee*, not a drop of white blood had been shed by the Nez Perce.

"We must face these things like adults, sister. The soldiers are here, and we have less than the time of one moon to gather our herds and cross the mighty Kahmuenem, the Snake, to the place General Howard and Agent Monteith have ordered us." With a fatalism too old for his years, Yellow Moccasin shrugged his shoulders and, dismounting, led Rabbit Ears a short way from the tepee to stake him out.

Takseen was bewildered and not a little frightened by the thought of crossing the mighty torrent that divided their Oregon valley from Idaho. The order giving her people only one month to locate the widely dispersed herds and make the crossing was indeed cruel, for many lives would be lost in attempting such a foolhardy act. No one crossed the Kahmuenem when it was swollen with snow water from the mountains. Many weeks would pass before it would be fordable.

Darkness had fallen when she heard the angry voices of the young men raised in argument at the center of the camp. She drew near the edge of the fire, joining other curious women at the perimeter of the angry crowd. In the firelight Takseen could make out the faces of Buffalo Robe, Yellow Wolf, nephew of Chief Joseph, Going Alone, Rattle on Blanket, Five Wounds, Rainbow, and many others among the handsome young men of the band. Their faces showed a fierceness that was frightening in the firelight, and she shivered in the early-evening chill. Some faces still bore the paint of the past week's Council at Lapwai where the old Dreamer, Toohoohoolzote had been imprisoned by General

Howard as a result of his protests. The young men were violently opposed to such treatment.

Ollokut, brother of Chief Joseph, stepped forward, commanding their attention. Taller than his brother, Ollokut was a remarkable athlete and a fine hunter who had earned the respect of his fellows. The angry voices hushed momentarily, giving attention to the man whose normally smiling face was no longer full of laughter. Ollokut raised his hand somberly, the vermillion stripe in the part of his hair giving testimony to the recent Council at Lapwai where the warriors had displayed their paint.

"You have seen the white soldiers in our valley," he said. "Would you shed the blood of your wives and your children? Would you lose your own lives, leaving your young ones fatherless?"

The young men stirred in disagreement. "A man who would leave his land is a man who would leave his own mother. Better that our bones and our blood return to the soil which gave us birth."

Before another voice could be raised in assent or in protest, there was a disturbance at the edge of the crowd. A stir of excitement was visible as the old *tewat*, the medicine man Toohoohoolzote, strode to the center of the gathering.

"He has been freed by General Howard," the old women chorused and wagged their heads in anticipation, for there would be a tirade to stir the blood of the young men.

Anger and resentment gleamed in the eyes of the old Dreamer at his recent imprisonment.

Takseen, taking all this in from her spot among the women, kept her eyes on Buffalo Robe, to watch his reaction.

In a haranguing voice Toohoohoolzote began. "General Howard would have us run like dogs from the place of our birth. We are not dogs; we are the *numipu*, the People, and we will not leave the valley where lie the bones of our fathers and our mothers. General Howard has dared to arrest me and imprison me when I protested his order. General Howard is the dog, and only blood will erase the insult he has thrown upon us."

There was a chorus of "aahs" from the restless ones who agreed that bloodshed was the only answer. Buffalo Robe stood unmoved before the powerful diatribe that issued from the lips of Toohoohoolzote.

"I will tell you the words of Agent Monteith and General Howard. They say to me that a medicine man who counsels disobedience must be punished. And I say to them, 'You white people get together, measure the earth and then divide it.' Agent Monteith replies, 'The law says you must come to the reservation. The law is made in Washington. We don't make it.' "

Toohoohoolzote raised a clenched fist. " 'The earth is part of my body,' I said to him. 'I never gave up the earth.' Then I asked General Howard, 'What person pretends to divide the land and put me on it?' "

"I am the person. I stand here for the President."

The fire did not leave the eyes of Toohoohoolzote, and there were nods of agreement as the young men said to one another, "They cannot do this to us."

Seeing that the feelings of the young warriors were strongly with him, the *tewat* continued. "At last I said to General Howard, 'Are you the Great Spirit? Did you make the world? Did you make the sun? Did you make the rivers to run for us to drink? Did you make the grass to grow? Did you make all these things that you talk to us as though we were boys? If you did, then you have the right to talk to us as you do.' "

Satisfied at the shouts of agreement, Toohoohoolzote sat down and let his words take effect.

A respectful silence fell as Joseph, who had been standing quietly aside, asked to be heard. His handsome, unsmiling face was more somber than usual.

"Our valley is filled with soldiers. We have few rifles and less ammunition. The federal soldiers have artillery and gatling guns. Would you have us fight them with bow and arrow? We are no match for the soldiers, and who would come to our aid if we began to fight? The Crows, the Blackfeet, the Sioux, all would join General Howard against us. Our women and children and our old people would suffer the most.

"There is no choice," he concluded sadly, "we must do as the white man's government tells us. For this task we must have strong hearts. Rather than have war, I would give up my country. I would give up my father's grave. I would give up everything rather than have the blood of white men upon the hands of my people.

"Tomorrow the boys must complete the roundup of the wandering horses and cattle while the women make preparations for the journey across the *Kahmuenem*. I have spoken."

There were grumbling remarks among many. "We will defy your authority," Hohots, the Grizzly Bear, retorted. "We will not leave."

Takseen saw Joseph turn sadly away. He could only attempt to persuade, for he did not have sole authority. What the final decision would be was still uncertain. She respected the wisdom of Joseph and knew he would not lightly make the heartbreaking decision he had expressed that night. She was glad to see that Buffalo Robe had not joined the grumblers, though her own feelings were mixed.

She returned sadly to her tepee, joining Yellow Moccasin and their parents, Lone Coyote and his younger wife, Gray Deer. Like her daughter, Gray Deer was comely, though her slender shape had not returned since the birth of the infant who lay contentedly on a buffalo robe within the tepee. Broken Wing, with the privilege of an old woman and the first wife, was already asleep in the corner, making small muttering noises in her throat.

Yet sleep would not come to the others; they were looking deep within their hearts for strength to accept the difficult days that lay ahead.

Takseen was not surprised that the vigil of the flageolet player was not repeated that night. Thus she was startled when a voice broke the silence.

"May I enter?"

Lone Coyote nodded assent and Gray Deer raised the flap of the tepee to allow Buffalo Robe admittance.

Lone Coyote offered him a place to be seated, and Buffalo Robe respectfully addressed the parents with no preliminaries.

"I have come about the matter of your daughter's hand in marriage." He gazed steadily at Lone Coyote, his head high.

Takseen sat in a dim corner of the tepee, taking all this in with pounding heart. Buffalo Robe glanced her way only once, then went about the serious business of winning her parents' consent.

"Have you asked the girl?" Lone Coyote inquired bluntly.

"She has not said she will become my wife."

"Why don't you ask her?"

Takseen raised her hand to her mouth in sudden embarrassment. She was not prepared to be put to the question.

"Takseen, little Willow, will you agree to be the wife of Buffalo Robe?" the handsome young man addressed her, his finely chiseled features expressing little feeling, but his eyes filled with love.

Takseen looked at the floor modestly and hesitated only a moment. "You have my consent."

"What have you to offer her?" the practical Lone Coyote asked.

Buffalo Robe, smiling now, said earnestly, "My father and his father before him were respected men. I come from a family of much honor. I have many horses, for there is wealth aplenty in the valley of the Winding Water."

"When do you wish to marry her if I give my consent?"

"These are troubled times. My heart says, in one moon, but if we must cross the mighty *Kahmuenem* and settle on the reserve of the Clearwater, I should say we will wait two moons."

Lone Coyote consulted Gray Deer for the first time, exchanging quiet remarks. He stood and Buffalo Robe followed suit, standing a head higher than Takseen's father. "My son," the old man said, "you have our favor to the match."

Buffalo Robe was visibly relieved, and he exchanged a smile with Takseen, whose modesty prevented her from coming forward to embrace him as she longed in her heart to do.

Taking the initiative, her betrothed approached her in two strides and put one strong arm about her shoulders, at the same time enclosing a gift within her palm. "This is for luck," he murmured.

Then, turning to the parents, Buffalo Robe said formally, "I thank you both for the promise of the hand of your daughter. We shall talk together soon. *Taz alago.* Good-by." So saying, he squeezed Takseen's slender hand and was gone.

She opened her fingers, revealing the gift he had enclosed within her hand. A lovely moss agate hung from a leather thong. Looking closely, she saw that the pattern of the stone closely resembled an owl, symbol of her personal *wyakin*, her attending spirit.

"Aah," she thought happily, "I shall treasure this gift all my life," and she placed it around her neck.

In one corner of the tepee came the sounds of muffled giggles from Yellow Moccasin, who could never refrain from teasing his sister; in the other corner the snores of Broken Wing increased in volume in an unsatisfactory attempt to feign sleep.

5

The first rays of sunlight were slanting across the valley of the Winding Water when the sun herald rode through the village shouting his morning ritual.

"I wonder if everyone is up! It is morning. We are alive, so thanks be! Rise up! Look about! Go see the horses, lest a wolf have killed one! Thanks be that the children are alive!—and you, older men!—and you, older women!—also that your friends are probably alive in other camps. But elsewhere there are probably those who are ill this morning, and therefore the children are sad, and therefore their friends are sad."

So saying, he returned to his lodge to wait, like the other men, for his breakfast. The women stood before their tepees, stirring the dying embers of the fires, creating a spot for their men to warm themselves on that crisp morning late in May, 1877.

Flames licked at the kettle while Takseen stirred the thick kouse gruel for the morning meal. She flavored it with wild onion gathered from the hills. Her mother, Gray Deer, sat nearby, contentedly nursing the infant, enjoying for a moment a sense of happiness at her daughter's betrothal. She took much pride in her beautiful daughter, who had taken over many of her tasks since the baby's birth. Gray Deer, no longer a young woman, having thirty-two winters, had never regained her strength from the difficult labor, and was grateful for her daughter's help. She watched Takseen pat together some small cakes flavored with the last of the serviceberries from the previous summer.

Then Gray Deer strapped the chubby baby in her *tekash*, her cradleboard, and the men gathered for a bowl of gruel and a serviceberry cake warm from the fire.

After breakfast Yellow Moccasin untethered Rabbit Ears and led him toward a boisterous group of young boys who were preparing to go into the hills in search of the wandering stock. Only a few of the older boys had appeared for the task, and Takseen saw Joseph walk throughout the camp, seeking out the reluctant ones.

She watched as he laid a hand on Grizzly Bear's shoulder and looked into his eyes. Hohots, the arrogant Grizzly Bear, could not withstand Joseph's look, and he turned away. One by one Joseph approached the young men of his band who had not accepted his decision, laying a gentle hand on their shoulders. One by one they nodded assent as he searched their eyes and their hearts, feeling their pain and sharing it with them.

Soon only the old men were left, while all those who could ride a horse were out searching for the scattered stock that represented the wealth of their band.

Takseen and the women repeated the job of the day before, searching for the camas roots and cleaning and drying their harvest.

That day passed like the subsequent ones, as the people went about their preparations with heavy hearts. The only bit of happiness for Takseen was the amulet that lay close to her heart and the promise of marriage that it represented.

Daily the herd of rounded-up stock increased, and it became necessary to add more attendants to safeguard the stock day and night. Yellow Moccasin won this coveted position of helping tend the vast numbers of beautiful spotted-rumped Appaloosas and the other horses and ponies whose sleek sides were filling out from the abundant grass in the valley.

The cattle too looked fat and healthy, and nearly all the cows and mares boasted handsome offspring that quickly gained in size and strength from the abundant pasturage.

Time was running short. It was already the first week in June, and those animals as yet uncollected must be left to the greedy white scavengers who roamed the valley.

The week began with unseasonal rains that made the crossing of the Kahmuenem an even greater threat. Takseen felt a sense of ominous foreboding in keeping with the leaden skies. For sixteen years she had known nothing but the beauty of that valley—bunch grass and sage, meandering streams and lofty mountain peaks. In her heart she knew that parting with the land was wrong, but she was powerless to do anything else. Even her obstinate friend Pale Moon had reluctantly agreed that there was no other choice.

But Takseen was young enough to be hopeful; with a good marriage in the near future she was content to see what the next months would bring, although her heart grieved at the parting.

It was the last morning in the valley of the Winding Water, and the usually joyful message of the sun herald was not unmixed with sorrow.

"It is morning and we are alive, so thanks be! Rise up

and look about! There will be other sunrises after this day!
Do not be disheartened, for we are well and strong, and our
families and our possessions are gathered about us! Be strong
of heart for *Hunyewat* is also in the land of the Clearwater.
Rise up! So be it!"

There was no smell of cooking fires that morning. A
sense of sober urgency superimposed itself upon the Wallamwatkins as they hastened to pack their lodge poles.

The first two days of the trip were much alike. Takseen
and Gray Deer rode astride two chestnut mares, their favorite
saddle mounts from among Lone Coyote's respectable herd.
The baby gurgled contentedly in the *tekash* strapped to her
mother's back.

Takseen had many free moments to visit with Pale Moon
as the girls rode along, helping to drive the pack train piled
high with household goods. Yellow Moccasin traveled behind
with the main horse herd, helping guard it from marauders.

The sun was approaching its zenith on the second day
when Buffalo Robe, who had been traveling behind with
the other warriors, overtook the column. His eyes had been
scanning the women on horseback for a glimpse of his betrothed, and he saw her leaving the pack train with her
friend Pale Moon. He turned his horse sharply and followed.

The women made frequent berry-picking stops along the
way, for the first of the succulent wild strawberries were
beginning to ripen. Lying in secret glades, they lured the
women from the monotonous plodding of the pack train like
the sweet promise of spring.

At first Takseen did not notice Buffalo Robe watching
her fondly from a distance. When at last he approached
her, she knew that he saw her lips stained with the sweet juice
of the berries. Pale Moon slipped away with a discreetness
that was unusual for her.

Buffalo Robe placed a finger across her juice-stained lips, then tasted of the sweetness. Takseen laughingly offered him a berry and in its sharing she felt a surge of pleasure for their future together.

His hand went to the amulet she wore close to her heart, and he studied it for a moment. Takseen felt her heart swell at the nearness of her loved one, and she looked with love, and a little trepidation, into his eyes.

"I found this stone beyond the shining mountains, in the land of the buffalo," he told her kindly. "It was lying along the banks of the Yellowstone, and when I saw the figure of the owl formed within the rock, I knew that it would one day be yours, and that you would one day be mine."

"The owl has brought me much good fortune," she affirmed. "I want you to know, though we have spoken little together, that I am well pleased to become your wife."

Her eyes said more than her lips, and they shared a warm embrace that would have been longer but for the gentle cough behind them. Pale Moon came into the clearing, ostensibly to retrieve her horse, which had wandered away. There was no mistaking the admiration in her round face as she stared a moment longer than necessary at the broad-shouldered Buffalo Robe with his square chin and finely shaped features. For once, words failed her, and she turned back to the main trail, one hand over her mouth, leading her errant horse behind her.

The moments passed too quickly for Takseen, who had much to say to the young man who had courted and won her, but there would be a lifetime to say all that was in her heart. Buffalo Robe had to return to his position with the warriors, she to watch over the pack animals as the procession wound slowly along the river valley.

Each day they made camp in the early afternoon, and the women scurried about unpacking and setting up the tepees, gathering wood, and hauling water. Moving from place to place within the valley had been commonplace, but there was a deep sense of finality about those two days' travel. Every step was one that would never be retraced; every step from the Wallowa left a painful imprint in the hearts of each Wallamwatkin. By the afternoon of the second day, the people of Joseph's band had reached the Kahmuenem, just above its confluence with the Imnaha.

Takseen's courage failed her at the sight of the angry yellow torrent boiling between the rocky walls, a quarter of a mile wide. The current swept past faster than a man could walk, stronger than the strongest swimmer. Several times she had crossed the Salmon, a formidable feat in itself, yet the fury of the Salmon was reduced to weak murmurings by the icy torrent that roared past on its journey toward what the *shoyapee* called Hell's Canyon.

Takseen was sick at the thought of the young foals and newborn calves who would be swept to instant death on the rocks the moment they entered the water. The young men were thinking the same thoughts, and again they began to grumble, cursing the wisdom of Joseph.

"Is there a choice?" Takseen heard him urging the reluctant ones. "Do you wish to return to our valley which a week ago was filled with white soldiers, a valley which by now is filled with settlers who waited like wolves to slip in before the dust of our passing had settled?"

The grumbling slackened as the men went about the necessity of fashioning rafts for the crossing, working in groups at the task.

Takseen helped cut poles of green willow the thickness of her thumb. She kept Buffalo Robe supplied with strong saplings for the frame of the raft.

He worked with his friend Black Elk and was joined by Yellow Moccasin, who had been relieved of his guard duties for the time being. They first stretched a buffalo hide, hair side up, flat on the ground. While one man bent the hide and poles up, the other lashed more bent poles to the top, forming a circular rim.

The afternoon passed quickly for Takseen, whose fear of the next day's crossing was somewhat assuaged by the opportunity to be near Buffalo Robe.

"Stay close to me tomorrow," he told her when the work was finished. "I will see you and your family safely across the river."

That night Takseen lay waiting for sleep. It was warm and there was an unaccustomed sultriness in the air. The booming of the water as it pounded against the rocks and swept down past the canyon walls was a constant reminder of the watery ordeal that faced them on the morrow.

She silently invoked her *wyakin*, the owl, her hand clutching the amulet that embodied its power. Her fear was not for her own safety so much as for that of her loved ones, and for the weak and helpless young stock that faced certain death at the crossing.

The morning arrived under gray skies. The air was heavy for the month of the Strawberry Moon, but the clouds held back the deluge that was building up, as if the heavens did not wish to further swell the overburdened stream beds.

The women struck camp and began to gather in an orderly fashion on the rocky banks of the river beside their mounds of household goods. The women and children with their possessions were to be ferried across first. Then the warriors would swim across on their most powerful mounts, driving the vast herd of horses and cattle before them.

"Over here!" Buffalo Robe shouted to Takseen above the roar of the water. She saw the tall figure astride his best horse, War Bonnet, who was dancing nervously alongside the raft. Lone Coyote loaded his wives and daughters into the raft, and

Yellow Moccasin did the work of two men lifting robes and clothing, baskets and kettles, into the raft.

Lone Coyote gazed at his three children, Takseen, Yellow Moccasin, and the infant as if he might not see them again. "Take care of the women, my son!"

Yellow Moccasin was startled. "I am not a *meopkowit*, a baby, to be ferried across the water with ancient grandmothers and babes in their cradleboards! I will ride with the men!" He protested indignantly.

"You are a man, my son. Of that I have no doubt, but your little pony Rabbit Ears, loyal though he is, could not safely carry you across the raging river."

Bowing to the will of his father, Yellow Moccasin reluctantly stepped in. Buffalo Robe and three other young men on strong horses would tow the raft, one to a corner. Stripped to only breechclouts, the four men guided their anxious horses into the swirling eddies in the lee of a large boulder, towing the raft between them.

Before Takseen could prepare herself for the ride, they were swept into the current. The horses struggled bravely while the riders urged on their seemingly futile efforts.

The roar of the river was overpowering. With only the thin hide of an animal separating the occupants from the river, they could feel its writhing contortions beneath them, like a living thing.

Takseen clutched the rim of the raft with one hand. With the other she held her infant sister tightly, for her mother's weakened condition made it difficult for Gray Deer to hold the child safely. Broken Wing sat stonily in her corner, surrounded by soaking blankets and buffalo robes, her lips moving in a silent entreaty to Hunyewat.

Slowly the wildly plunging raft and the others that had by then left shore gained way, yard by painful yard.

Takseen judged they had passed the halfway point, but

the strength of the angry Kahmuenem had in no way diminished. They rode well into the water, propelled by the feeble motions of the tiring horses; but at last they became part of a separate broad channel of yellow water that carried them closer to the far shore.

Takseen's heart pounded as she saw the great jagged boulders marking the water's edge. There was only one level point of land to provide a safe landing place on the rocky shore.

The men on horseback dug their feet into the horses' sides, willing them to safety with their last ounce of strength. Only yards from shore, the raft broke free of the grip of the current, entering the calmer area in which boils and eddies were more a match for the waning strength of the animals.

The horses were finally only belly deep and they dragged the raft the last short distance. Takseen gratefully stepped ashore, holding her hand out to Gray Deer, who tremblingly followed. The horses snorted and blew water from their noses, the muscles rippling along their sides as they panted and shook the icy water from their dripping flanks.

Buffalo Robe dismounted and Takseen wrapped a blanket about his naked shoulders. She leaned against him gratefully, lending him her body's warmth, then dried the drops of water still clinging to his skin.

"I'm grateful to you for guiding us safely across," she told him.

"I promised no harm would come to you." He smiled, looking into the depths of her black eyes.

Other exhausted teams were dragging rafts onto the sandy shelf where the first had landed. Takseen reached for wet and trembling children, taking them from their mothers' arms as the mothers stepped unsteadily ashore. For all the fearful moments of the dreadful crossing, there was not one tear from the stoical children. A few of the older ones seemed to have reveled in the excitement of crossing the raging river.

As the morning wore on and the rafts made a second dangerous crossing, all heads were miraculously accounted for among the women, children, and old people. Only the stock remained on the Oregon side, with Joseph and the warriors to drive them.

Takseen anxiously scanned the far shore for a glimpse of the animals. The power of the current had carried the rafts hundreds of yards downstream from the point they had put in. Takseen could not make out individuals, but she saw the animals bunched on higher ground, milling around under the watchful eye of the guards. Though she could hear nothing but the booming of the water, she knew the cows would be bawling frantically to their calves, the mares restlessly pawing the earth with an anxious eye to their foals.

She saw a raised hand signal the beginning of the drive. With a blind headlong surge, the cattle and horses took to the water in a grand rush. The ponies and horses were in the lead, and before they could break away, the cattle followed.

The sounds of panic could not reach her, but Takseen felt them in her heart as the weaker ones rapidly fell away from the group of stronger swimmers. Then all were lost from view as a solid wall of water poured from the lowering sky in a sudden cloudburst.

Minutes passed and the bodies of little calves and colts began sweeping past Takseen's vantage point, their helpless bodies dashing upon the jagged rocks of either bank.

They drowned by hundreds in the wild rapids, not only the young, but the smaller and weaker of the full-grown animals.

The survivors stumbled up the banks for a hundred yards in either direction from Takseen, bawling and neighing pathetically. The mares looked anxiously about for their young, unable to comprehend the full scope of the disaster that had befallen them.

With sickened heart, Takseen turned her eyes to the river again. The violent cloudburst had passed and the sun was breaking through a patch of blue. A fat sleek pony swept past, struggling futilely in the current, its eyes rolling wide with fear. She heard her brother call out, "Rabbit Ears! This way. This way, Rabbit Ears!" The pony struggled briefly at the sound of the voice, but its strength was spent and its head went under, closing from view the wild-eyed look it had cast ashore. Seconds later the battered body washed ashore, but there was no life left in the gallant little pony. Takseen's heart went out to Yellow Moccasin, who ran to his pony and stood unashamedly weeping over the body of his beloved Rabbit Ears. Rivulets of water ran off its coat, joining the tears that fell upon it.

The grim-eyed warriors struggled onto shore, followed by Joseph. The sag in the chieftain's shoulders was visible, as if he carried the weight of all the crushed and battered bodies upon himself.

No one spoke of the tragedy, but looked to the hundreds of stalwart animals who had made the crossing, gathering them together and rejoicing over the survival of their favorites.

The task of drying the family's belongings and setting up camp fell to Takseen. Yellow Moccasin refused to help round up the surviving animals, so broken-hearted was he at the loss of Rabbit Ears. Takseen felt his loss keenly, and did not think him any less a man for his display of emotion.

The entire band went about the routine of setting up camp mechanically, lost in their own sorrowful emotions. Some cursed Joseph, others Agent Monteith for his arbitrary timing of the order to come to Lapwai.

The family took a light supper of jerked meat and fresh

berries, sharing a deep silence. It was broken by the sound
of a rider approaching. Looking up from her bowl, Takseen
saw Buffalo Robe astride War Bonnet. He was leading a
spirited young Appaloosa, rich brown in color with chestnut
spots across its white rump.

"Is Yellow Moccasin within?" he asked by way of greeting.

Gray Deer called the boy from the tepee. "Someone calls
you," she told him.

The dejected boy emerged, but his shoulders immediately
straightened at the sight of the warrior he most admired.

"Here is a present for you," Buffalo Robe told the boy,
bending over to pass the reins to him. "He cannot replace
Rabbit Ears, I know, but treat him well and he will be a
good mount for you. I call him Spotted Eagle." He smiled
at the boy. "A man needs a good horse."

Yellow Moccasin smiled proudly and words failed him.
He stroked Spotted Eagle's muzzle and spoke softly to him.
The boy's gratitude shown from his eyes.

Acknowledging the look with a nod, Buffalo Robe turned
on War Bonnet and rode away.

6

Tepahlewam was an ancient camp of the Nez Perce lying at the head of Rocky Canyon near Tolo Lake, only a few miles from the Lapwai reservation. It was to this resting place that Joseph's band of Wallamwatkins gathered for the two weeks remaining before they were to enter the confines of the reservation.

To this camp the other bands of non-treaty Nez Perce also came: Looking Glass's Asotins, White Bird's Lamtamas, and the people of Chief Toohoohoolzote's band.

Takseen had seldom seen such a great gathering of her people. In all there were about six hundred Nez Perce in camp, many of them old people, women, and children.

An air of festivity replaced the somberness following the tragic crossing of the Kahmuenem. The women, with a spirit of camaraderie, continued their camas harvest while the men gambled and held horse races, forgetting their troubles for the moment in the wildly competitive games. Carried away by high spirits and mock warplay, the young men fired playful shots at each other from beneath their horses' bellies.

Takseen saw little of Buffalo Robe during that week, for

the men argued night and day whether or not to fight. As he did earlier in Joseph's camp, Toohoohoolzote inflamed the hearts of the young men, inciting them to shed blood, but for the time being, the peacemaking efforts of Joseph and the other chiefs who did not want war prevailed.

On the eighth day Takseen looked up from the canvas where she was spreading camas bulbs to dry. Coming toward her with the awkward gait of one who is great with child was Joseph's wife, Toma Alwawinmi, or Springtime. Takseen was acquainted with the pretty young girl, for whom Joseph's concern had been growing as her time approached.

"Is the old one within?" Springtime nodded toward the tepee. Broken Wing, who was deaf only when she wanted to be, responded by her presence.

"My time is coming soon, old mother, and I would like to be assured of your skills of midwifery when I deliver."

The old woman was well pleased by the request, though in one part of her heart she wished to remain close to the parades and the boisterous arguing that had entertained her so the past week. The event of childbirth required the seclusion of the mother and her attendant in a special lodge some distance from the main village.

"When is the child coming?" Broken Wing asked.

"Very soon, I am certain. The child's movements have quieted and I have had pain ever since we crossed the Kahmuenem."

Broken Wing placed a clawlike hand on Springtime's abdomen, her experienced fingers judging the imminence of the infant's arrival.

She looked hard at Takseen. "My child, I will need your help. I am not so young as I used to be. If you assist me this time, your knowledge will ease your own deliveries when you give Buffalo Robe his sons."

So it was that Takseen spent the last week at Tepahlewam in the childbirth lodge, apart from the activities that would inevitably plunge her people into war.

Springtime did not deliver as soon as she had expected.

"It was the journey across the icy waters that brought on your pains," the old woman explained. "You're young and healthy and, thanks be to Hunyewat, the baby's heart still beats strongly."

Joseph had ridden with his brother Ollokut and a few chosen assistants across Mahsamyetten (Buzzard Mountain) to slaughter cattle below the Salmon River. The three women were left to pass the time alone. Broken Wing regaled them with legends and tales of their race.

On the second night in the childbirth tepee Broken Wing began the story of the creation of the Nez Perce people. It was a beloved old story and Takseen listened with the pleasure of familiarity while she sat by Springtime, bathing her forehead. The young woman was restless from pains that had been coming irregularly since sunset.

"Rest yourself, my dear," the old woman soothed. "You will be a mother before very long, but you are not the first, nor will you be the last. Every person on earth, even the *shoyapee*, was born in pain from the womb of its mother, even unto the beginning of our race."

Broken Wing turned from the perspiring Springtime and squatted before the small fire in the center of the tepee. Smoke curled idly upward toward the smokehole. Broken Wing's beady eyes stared intently into the fire and she began to chant in a hypnotic voice.

"In the Valley of the Kamiah, not too far from here, in a beautiful canyon, lies a mound as big as a hill. Perhaps you will see the mound before too long. It marks the spot where lay the heart of a great monster, a monster so large it filled the entire valley. The world was new and there were yet no people. The monster did not need to search for food, for he could draw in animals, great and small, for a distance of many miles, and swallow them alive. The creatures of the earth devised all methods to destroy this enemy of all beast-kind, for the valley was white with the bones of their friends. Only one among them dared to approach the dreaded animal. This was the coyote, for always, when he drew near, the creature shut his mouth tightly, saying, 'Go away!' One day, after the coyote had gathered some pitch pine and flint, he crept quietly up alongside the monster, and hit the shut mouth so that it opened with a jerk, and in a moment the brave little coyote was inside the great prison house. What a company he found there, the sick, dead, and dying!"

Not breaking the rhythm of the story, Broken Wing looked up and saw that her voice had taken effect and lulled Springtime to sleep. Sataisfied, she continued, "Soon with his pitch and flint he kindled a fire, and the smoke came puffing out of the mouth, ears, and nose of the monster. The little fellow inside ordered all yet alive to make their escape. The great white bear said he was not able to go, but finally went out through the ear gate. All this time the coyote was sawing away on the great heart with his flint, listening with delight to the sick groans of the dying beast.

"When all the captives were out and at liberty, there stood in the silence only the coyote and his friend the fox. What should be done with this great body? They finally decided to cut it in pieces, and from the pieces people the world. So the Blackfoot Indians were made from the feet, and the Crows and Flatheads from the head, and other tribes were made from other parts of the body and sent off to their own lands. The two friends were left alone.

"The fox, looking up and down the river said, 'Why, we have made no people for this beautiful valley, and nothing left to make them from.'"

" 'True,' said the coyote, 'nothing but a few drops of the heart's best blood left on my hands. Bring me some water from the river.'

"This was done. While the coyote washed his hands, he sprinkled the ground with blood and water, and lo! the noble Nez Perces sprang up."

Takseen smiled into the beady eyes of the old woman, who had not only lulled the distressed Springtime to sleep, but had reinforced Takseen's own pride in her people, sprung from the "heart's best blood." Perhaps this reserve on the Clearwater would not be so bad, for didn't Lapwai itself lie along the Clearwater?

Her thoughts were interrupted by a soft moan from Springtime. The girl's face registered pain, though she made no outcry as the contractions began to increase in frequency and intensity.

"What is happening now?" she breathed, her head tossing restlessly.

"All is as it should be, my child. Your water has broken. It is a sign that the baby is coming."

"How much longer?"

"Soon, little mother."

Takseen bathed the perspiring forehead, marveling at the process of birth she was witnessing. Broken Wing offered Joseph's wife a cup of strong brew. "Sip this. It will ease your suffering."

Takseen did not inquire into its contents. Broken Wing was entitled to retain the secrets of her trade as a respected midwife.

Springtime was panting then, gripping a hide-covered

stick within her hands and squeezing tightly with each pain.

"Joseph! Joseph!" she moaned when seized by a mighty contraction.

"Now! The baby's head is coming! Push with each pain," Broken Wing instructed.

Springtime did as she was told, triumphant then that birth was imminent.

"Push! Bear down!" Broken Wing urged. "The baby is coming." Takseen's fingers massaged the girl's forehead faster as her own excitement increased. To be present at such a miracle!

With strength Takseen didn't believe possible, the young girl bore down with a final contraction, groaning from the depths of her body.

A black-haired scalp appeared, followed by a lustily bawling, red and wrinkled infant, curled so tightly it resembled no more than a rabbit.

Broken Wing lifted the slippery baby for Springtime to see.

"You have a daughter, little one. Like you, she is a sign of the spring of the year." So saying, Broken Wing passed the child to Takseen while she cut the cord.

Takseen was overcome with wonder at the bawling miracle, who seemed perfect in every way, her eyes tightly shut against the unaccustomed world. Tears coursed down Takseen's cheeks just as tears of happiness sparkled in the eyes of the young mother.

"Joseph will not mind," Springtime whispered. "A girl child will be precious to him." She took the child from Takseen's arms and, trembling with wonderment, held it to her breast.

For two days Takseen attended Joseph's young wife. Her thoughts turned often to the day she would bear a child for her warrior. Perhaps by this time the following year she would be delivered of Buffalo Robe's son.

So absorbed was she in her private reverie that she was taken by surprise when Joseph stepped into the tepee toward sunset the second day following the baby's birth. Joseph's handsome face was taut with tension, and they all feared he was displeased because his child was not a son.

"See what we have, my husband." Springtime smiled up at him from her pallet. "You are not displeased?"

"You have made me proud," he comforted her, holding her wrists in his great hands. Then, with great tenderness, he lifted his tiny daughter and cradled her in the crook of his arm. He touched her petal-soft cheek with a tentative finger, then gazed through the open flap of the tepee. His expression was inscrutable, but Takseen saw enormous sadness reflected in his eyes. She started to leave, but Joseph stopped her.

"Stay," he commanded. "You will not have heard the evil news from the main camp." He paused and his shoulders slumped with weariness. He spoke with finality. "Our people are at war."

The women held their hands to their mouths in disbelief.

"You were apart from the main camp. You did not hear the wild talk of Toohoohoolzote, or the taunts of the old man who goaded Wahlitits into avenging his father's death at the hands of the *shoyapee*."

Joseph sat down and continued sadly. "Wahlitits and his two near-cousins, Red Moccasin Tops and Swan Necklace, with the taste of fire-water crazing their brains, went on a killing spree on Slate Creek. They murdered four or five white settlers."

Broken Wing spoke up, the privilege of her age allowing her to interrupt her chief. "Those young men are not of our band. We need not go to war because of those young evil-doers!"

"I wish that were so," Joseph said. "They were members of White Bird's band, but the blame will fall upon all of us. There is worse yet to tell. The three warriors, bragging of their feat, encouraged other men to join them. Today a group of seventeen committed more killings on the Salmon. These were bad acts. They mistreated women and children, killed fourteen or fifteen men and plundered houses."

For a moment the women were stunned into silence.

"What can we do?" Takseen ventured at last.

"Many of our people have already left. They have gone to Sapachesap, the cave on Cottonwood Creek. A few have fled to Lapwai. All of Looking Glass's people have gone to their old home on the Clearwater. The women have gardens there. The Asotins want no war.

"Look to your own," Joseph counseled Takseen. "Your people may have already left for Sapachesap. The old one can stay with my wife. We shall strike camp in the morning."

Takseen untethered her mare and rode back to the main camp. The flat, dry ridge that served as the traditional Tepahlewam camp was nearly deserted. Only a few lodges remained. Nowhere did she see the tepee of Lone Coyote.

The sound of her horse brought a lone warrior from his lodge. It was Buffalo Robe.

Takseen looked anxiously at him and dismounted. They stood in the last slanting rays of the sun, bathed in the muted pink reflections of the rocky ridge.

"I have the news you are seeking," Buffalo Robe informed her. His black eyes showed a strained expression as if he, like Joseph, feared the consequences of the rash acts the young men had committed. "Your family has moved on to the camp at Sapachesap. Your father said to stay with the old one and help Joseph's wife. When she can move, you will rejoin your people."

Takseen nodded. "I'm glad they didn't wait. These are indeed evil times. Last night a dream came to me which struck fear in my heart." She looked away from Buffalo Robe, across the ridge toward the distant mountains. Then she continued, "I felt myself made helpless as if crushed by a great weight. While I was lying on the ground, unable to move, an owl fell lifelessly to my feet. I was able to raise myself only enough to examine the limp body and pull the shaft of an arrow from its body. Then the arrow in my hand dissolved, changing into a rifle such as the long knives carry. There was blood on the rifle and blood on my hands." She shuddered. "I don't know what to make of such a dream, but I can only feel that it was a sign of evil."

"I won't let harm come to you, little Willow," Buffalo Robe reassured her. He boosted her onto her mare and clasped her hand for a moment. "I will follow when you travel to Sapachesap."

"Joseph said he would strike camp in the morning."

"Then I will go with you tomorrow. Look now to Joseph's wife. She needs you, and you can learn from her," he said, smiling for the first time. "You too will be a mother some day. You must learn how to bear fine sons and daughters for your husband."

The troubled look in Takseen's eyes disappeared for a moment as she envisioned herself the proud mother of Buffalo Robe's children. "Those days will be better days than these. I hope we live to see them." She waved good-by and returned to Joseph's lodge.

7

Joseph remained quietly at Sapachesap on Cottonwood Creek. The camp no longer numbered 600. All of Looking Glass's Asotins were on the Clearwater. The smaller camp was composed primarily of Joseph's and White Bird's people.

Takseen divided her time between Springtime, who no longer required much care, and her mother, Gray Deer, who lay sick with a fever. Takseen was saddened to see her mother growing more frail. Her baby sister, too, was suffering from her mother's lessened milk supply.

To this worry was added the growing tension in the camp. Several days had passed when Nez Perce scouts brought word of the approach of white soldiers. Mounted soldiers followed by walking troops were only a few days' march from Sapachesap. Takseen knew from the men's talk that the long knives were accompanied by mule teams hauling the thunder birds, the great howitzers. The white men would also have gatling guns which spoke from many barrels, sending death and destruction in their wake. These resources of men and supplies vastly overshadowed the meager fifty rifles owned by Nez Perce warriors. The combined fighting strength of the Indian bands numbered only seventy. The rest were noncombatants.

That war was inevitable was being assured by small groups of young warriors whose violent attacks on settlers expressed the pent-up hatred that could no longer be contained. Those few men exterminated several families, set fire to grain and buildings, and drove off the settlers' stock. The young men behaved like trapped animals, and all their fury and swallowed pride were released in a score of vengeful acts.

Buffalo Robe, showing more restraint and wisdom than his fellows, refrained from taking part in the killings. He sided with Joseph, though there was no longer much attempt at peacemaking. Like Joseph, he thought it more prudent to save what ammunition they had until the soldiers arrived.

Through Buffalo Robe, Takseen learned of Joseph's long-range plan, an alternative to surrender. They would attempt to wear down the white enemy and draw them far from their supply sources until the Indians could replenish their own ammunition and rifles by capturing the enemy's. If they could defeat the whites, perhaps Joseph could lead his people to a new country where the Wallamwatkins would be left in peace. This was the dream that Takseen held in her heart while the acts of the hotheaded young men made such a dream less and less likely.

Joseph, with great concern for his little family as well as for all the other noncombatants, determined to move closer to the base of White Bird Canyon, where the Indians could better defend their position.

They made the move simultaneously with word that Captain David Perry with ninety cavalry had left Fort Lapwai on the middle day of the Strawberry Moon.

The new camp was at the base of a three-thousand-foot canyon that rose in steep grassy ascents, slope on slope, ridge on rounded hill to a lofty plateau above. The hills were bisected by lateral ravines that provided pack trails in and out of the canyon. At that time of year the normally brown slopes were green with a fresh growth of grass. The campsite was located behind a low hill where the village would be concealed from the white soldiers, who must approach from the plateau above.

The first day in the new camp at the base of White Bird Canyon passed in a state of unrest. The next day would bring the soldiers, and with their arrival would come the first battle the Nez Perce had ever fought against the whites. No one doubted the Nez Perce would give battle. If Joseph still held out hope for reconciliation, he kept it within his heart.

Yellow Moccasin was at a fever pitch of excitement, not yet old enough to join the warriors but too old in his own eyes to be sheltered with the women and children.

Lone Coyote cautioned Takseen, "Watch out for that rascal tomorrow, that he does not rush out to do battle with the long knives."

"Must you fight, Father?" Takseen asked. In her eyes Lone Coyote was an aging elder who should live out his last years in peace rather than join the abler young men in battle.

"Of course I will fight. I am not a feeble old man, so wipe the pity from your eyes," he ordered her. Then softening a little, he joked, "If I am so feeble, how does it happen that you have an infant sister?"

Takseen smiled. "I did not say you were feeble, my father, but I fear for your safety and for the safety of all the young men."

"Don't worry about me, or for Buffalo Robe. He is a buffalo hunter and they make the finest warriors. Go tend your mother now, and mind what I said about Yellow Moccasin." Takseen felt a surge of affection as she turned from her father to do his bidding.

The deep canyon was still in shadow when the first weak rays of sunlight outlined the forms of men on horseback starting down the rugged defile.

Yellow Moccasin brought word to the tepee that Ollokut had spied the treaty Nez Perce riding with the soldiers.

Suddenly the whole village was awakened when Chuslum

Mox Mox (Yellow Bull), Joseph's sentinel, galloped through the village shouting "Soldiers! The soldiers are coming!" Dashing back and forth through the village he ordered, "Take down the lodges. Load them on the ponies. Take cover behind the butte." He shouted and pointed to a sheltered position farther down the canyon until the dazed villagers began to comply with his orders.

"You, boy!" he shouted to Yellow Moccasin. "Get the others and drive the spare pony herd downriver behind the bluff."

Yellow Moccasin was suddenly stunned by the panic of activity around him. Not until Chuslum Mox Mox lashed him sharply on the shoulder with his reins did the boy move into action.

His head cleared and he jumped on the back of Spotted Eagle and dashed full speed for the ponies. Lone Coyote meanwhile armed himself with bow and arrow and mounted his best pony, a sturdy gray Appaloosa. "You will be safe behind the bluffs," he flung over his shoulder to his women, who were dismantling the tepee.

There were screams and shouts as the women struck camp in a flurry of excitement. Takseen felt a brief surge of panic until Buffalo Robe rode by, stopping for a quick word of comfort. He was stripped for battle, wearing only a breechclout and moccasins. He carried a rifle and two cartridge belts, one around his waist, the other across his left shoulder and under his right arm. War Bonnet danced with excitement under him and Takseen placed a quieting hand on his muzzle.

"There is no cause for worry. We will give the long knives a beating today!" Buffalo Robe told her. All the fury he had felt at the whites, so long suppressed, was at last being given vent. His confidence was catching and Takseen felt his surging excitement.

"Take this for luck," she urged, pressing her owl amulet upon him. "Let my *wyakin* add its protection to you today."

He placed the moss agate around his neck and they exchanged a loving look. "May your life be preserved today," she told him. "We can't be cheated of the day when we will be man and wife."

He nodded. "Take care of your mother, little Willow," and he was soon out of sight.

The chaos of the camp became orderly under the direction of Mox Mox. The spare pony herd was concealed behind the bluffs downriver and the women followed with their laden pack ponies.

The minutes passed agonizingly slowly, for from that distance nothing could be seen. The first sounds of firing reached their ears indistinctly.

Takseen made Gray Deer comfortable in a shady spot beside the stream. Her mother's fever had abated somewhat, but the tension of the moment did little to increase her milk supply. The baby tugged at her breast with impatience.

Broken Wing was still with Joseph's wife, and Yellow Moccasin was with the pony herd, so the women had nothing to do but wait tensely for news of the battle.

There was another burst of firing, and the sound of war whoops carried across the distance. Just then Yellow Moccasin galloped past on Spotted Eagle. He was leading a pony behind him.

"Where are you going, little brother?" Takseen called.

"Buffalo Robe may need a spare mount. I am taking it to him."

"Don't be foolish, you *meopkowit*. You'll be killed. A battlefield's no place for a baby."

Her insult had the wrong effect, and Yellow Moccasin dug his heels into the pony's ribs, pounding out of sight around the bend.

Gray Deer's eyes widened with fear for her only son. "Stop him, daughter!" she pleaded. Takseen jumped on her mare and lashed her into a gallop.

She rounded the second bluff and the sound of firing was loud in her ears. She saw Yellow Moccasin leading the pony up a narrow ravine, but Buffalo Robe was nowhere in sight, and the boy prudently took cover behind a cluster of sage and boulders. With her head low, Takseen galloped across the intervening space, then led her mare up the steep ravine to Yellow Moccasin's hiding place.

They had a good vantage point to witness the battle. At first she could make no sense of the moving columns of men, but slowly a pattern emerged.

Toward the upper ridges of the bare slopes of the canyon three groups of cavalry advanced, but their lines were ragged and a dozen blue-clad bodies were already sprawled on the ground. Scattered among the uniformed cavalry were non-soldier citizens.

Takseen heard the firing of the Nez Perce sharp-shooters before she saw them. Slowly she picked them out from their concealed spots within the ravines above her. Their marksmanship was deadly accurate. A dozen riderless horses were tossing their heads in panic, rushing up the steep slope to regain the plateau above. Here and there the lines of soldiers were breaking. Takseen's heart pounded as she took in their confusion.

Indian heads bobbed from behind boulders and brush and their marksmanship began to take effect. On the left, White Bird's mounted warriors outflanked the citizen's column, wounding two and causing the others to break and run. The warriors occupied the knoll and swept over it, firing on the soldiers below.

"Look!" cried Yellow Moccasin to his sister. He pointed to a large herd of loose ponies being driven through the soldiers' ragged lines. Among them were concealed probably twenty warriors who caused havoc among the already confused troops.

The din of the battle had swelled. The long knives had lost their trumpeters and the officers' shouted orders fell on heedless ears. The stampeding Indian ponies and the soldiers' riderless horses added to the wild disorder.

Through the smoke of the firing, Takseen spotted Buffalo Robe. His figure was indistinct from that distance, but she couldn't mistake his prancing horse, War Bonnet.

The Indians were leaving the ravines and occupying the soldiers' positions as the rout became general and the warriors pursued the enemy to the higher ridges. There was a mad rush among the soldiers for their horses. The officers continued to shout, but the men would not re-form their lines.

Buffalo Robe was with a group of braves who doggedly pursued a retreating group of fourteen mounted men. Takseen kept her eyes on that action. The minutes wore on while the defenders bravely held their position, slowly progressing to higher ridges. For two hours the soldiers repulsed attack after attack. Buffalo Robe's cartridges were spent, but Takseen saw him rearm himself with a rifle and ammunition from a fallen soldier. She found herself grudgingly admiring the courage of those few pursued soldiers while all around them there was general panic among their comrades.

The activity was taking place high above Takseen and Yellow Moccasin, who remained glued to their spot. The battle had been going on for nearly four hours, judging by the sun, when the last soldiers gained the summit, disappearing across the plateau, still carrying on a running battle with the Indians.

Takseen could count more than a score of fallen soldiers. She knew there were more that she could not see. In one ravine an entire group had been cut off in a cul-de-sac.

Penned in by the blind canyon wall, they had fought until the last soldier fell dead.

"Let us take the news to camp," Yellow Moccasin cried triumphantly when the action had disappeared over the rim of the plateau. "What a victory!"

They stretched their limbs, cramped from lying so long behind the boulders, and mounted their ponies.

"I won't rest until Buffalo Robe and Father are safely back in camp."

"Don't worry, sister!" Yellow Moccasin boasted as if he had participated in the fight. "The white soldiers cannot harm us. Our medicine was strong today."

Takseen did not doubt she had seen an Indian victory, but she trembled nevertheless at the violence she had witnessed. An easy victory now, but what would the next day bring, and the day after that?

There was a great victory celebration in camp that night. The flames leaped high as warriors danced to the insistent drumming of the *tewats*. Painted bodies leaped against the background of flames, while the excited exclamations of the women and children filled the air.

Yellow Moccasin danced and whooped with the warriors in a triumphant frenzy. Gray Deer had forgiven him the worry he had caused by his headstrong refusal to stay in camp.

"You'd think the youngster had tasted blood today," Buffalo Robe observed to Takseen. He had not joined in the general celebration but kept his thoughts solemnly to himself.

"You're sad tonight, of all nights," Takseen told him. "They say there has never been such a defeat as the long knives suffered today—thirty-three dead, while none of our warriors were lost."

"That may be true, little Willow, but what is to happen

now? We have drunk of the white man's blood. Now they will never let us live in peace." There was a strained look in his eyes. "Joseph thinks we should slip away before General Howard can send reinforcements."

"But where will we go?"

"We must go beyond the buffalo country. There will be much fighting. Perhaps we will have peace only if we escape to the grandmother's land where Sitting Bull found refuge."

"That would take many moons. How can we travel so far with all our people, fighting the long knives all the way?"

"I do not know, little Willow," Buffalo Robe answered sadly. "It will be a dangerous journey."

8

Matthew Moss nervously shuffled a pile of completed government forms. A slight breeze came through the open window of his office, stirring the edges of the papers strewn about his desk. For the hundredth time that day he stared at the white walls of his office, bare except for maps of his forest district.

The young men of his crew sat on the porch steps, idly swatting the last of a six-week scourge of gnats. The fire danger was low since the big rain three days earlier, and they were enjoying their first leisure moments since the season had begun.

"Rusty," Matt called to his assistant.

A young red-haired man in a forest-service uniform left the porch and entered the office, letting the screen door slam behind him.

"Rusty," Matt said, "you're going to have to cover for me. I've got to hike into Moose Meadow Hill and check on a young girl camping alone. She should have checked in with the station by now."

"A young girl, huh?" Rusty said with a wink. "I thought you'd been a mite restless this week."

Matt felt surprise that anyone should have noticed his preoccupation. "Well, her fire permit's expired," he explained gruffly.

Katy had been on his mind more than once in the past few days, especially since the big storm three days earlier.

He left his desk, motioning for Rusty to sit down. "That report's all signed and ready to go. Maybe you can get it addressed and ready to send out with the supply truck." He went into the storeroom saying, "Thanks, Rusty. I'll be back by noon tomorrow at the latest."

Matt filled his canteen and grabbed the rucksack he always kept packed. He tossed them onto the seat of the forest-service pickup and drove away from the station.

His ranger station was the largest one in the area, providing a base for the firefighters and for the helicopter that sat idle on its grassy enclosure. Matt forced the pickup up over three miles of steep switchbacks climbing through a forest of lodgepole pines, then dropping over the ridge to the west side of the mountain. He bounced over four more miles of rough forest-service road strewn with boulders. When he parked the pickup at the junction with Moose Meadow Hill trail, he was still four miles from Katy's campsite.

Although Matt covered the steep trail in less than an hour and a half, it was noon before he entered the large upland meadow.

He scanned the area where Katy had been camping. The site was deserted and Matt's heart, which had not pounded with the exertion of the climb, was pounding when he saw that Katy's equipment had been scattered and ravaged by an animal.

"Katy!" he called, cupping his hands to his mouth. His voice sounded empty calling into the vastness of forest and meadow, for there was no answer. "Katy!" he called again. He listened quietly for several moments, but there was no response. He examined the ground more closely for some sign of what had happened. The tarp was shredded and the pack lay on its side, great tears showing where there had been zippered pockets. Plastic sacks, toilet articles, and clothing were scattered about. Mixed among them were empty foil pouches that had held her food.

All the telltale marks of a marauding bear were there. Yet, although everything edible or even smellable had been consumed, there was no sign of a struggle. Matt figured Katy had probably been absent from camp when the bear had performed its deviltry. What made Matt most uneasy was the fact that Katy had apparently not yet returned to discover the damage, and the camp had been ravaged at least a day earlier, possibly two.

He grew more nervous as he tried to piece together what had happened. All of Katy's equipment seemed to be there, even her sleeping bag. Then he remembered the bright orange poncho she had rigged for shelter over her sleeping bag; it was nowhere in sight. Could it be that she had taken it with her for protection from the rain the day of the storm and had gotten hurt some distance from camp?

Matt squeezed his eyes shut in concentration, trying to put himself in her place. Maybe she'd been looking for a favorite trapping spot of her great-grandpa's. Perhaps she'd taken the journal into the hills to read. That day he'd startled her as she was changing into dry clothing, she'd just come down from the ridge above.

Without stopping for lunch, Matt began his search. He scanned the meadow area with his binoculars, then headed for the top of the ridge, where he knew she'd been that previous time. If nothing else, he would at least get a good overview of the country from the rocky outcrop at the summit. With his high-powered binoculars he might be able to spot the bright orange of her poncho if she was anywhere nearby.

He climbed up the forested slope, his path lit by bright patches of sunlight. He quickly arrived at the ridge only a hundred feet above Katy's campsite.

His speculation about the myriad things that could have befallen her was getting out of hand. Even though they'd had only two conversations together, an intense attraction had drawn him to the pretty, dark-haired, blue-eyed girl. He was already blaming himself for whatever had happeend to her.

His feelings of guilt and worry were interrupted by a noisy fluttering. He looked into the tree above him, where a little brown owl stretched its wings on a low branch. Then it flew off toward the rocky outcrop. Matt thought it strange daytime behavior for an owl. Perhaps he'd disturbed its slumber. Then a shiver crept along his spine as he remembered Katy's strange dream and the owl that had promised to guide her on a mission.

He didn't have far to look. The owl lit on the branch of a fallen tree that had obviously come down in the recent storm. There beneath its branches lay a bright spot of orange, totally inert.

In a moment Matt was kneeling beside the still figure, and he pulled away the poncho. Katy was lying on her stomach, one leg distorted in an unnatural position, but possibly unbroken. Worst of all was a head wound where she'd been hit by a heavy branch that had grazed the side of her head. She lay deathly still.

He picked up her hand and it was clammy to the touch, but there beneath his fingers, he felt the thready movements of a faint pulse. She was alive!

"Thank God," Matt said softly. "Katy, Katy, can you hear me? It's Matt." She didn't stir from her unconscious state. "You're going to be all right, Katy. We'll get the chopper in here and you'll be safe in no time."

While he talked, Matt was unpacking first-aid materials. He cleansed the bruises on her face and head where she had fallen against the rocks, still keeping an anxious finger on her pulse. He did not like the faintness of it or the feel of her skin. Matt felt the presence of death, and he looked to the owl as if for reassurance. It still sat above him, blinking in the harsh sunlight. When it took flight it circled once over Katy's unconscious body before disappearing. With its departure the heavy sensation of a death presence lifted, and Matt finished his ministrations and wrapped Katy in a blanket.

"Katy, please understand, I have to leave you for a short while. I'll radio the station from my pickup, and before I can hike back up this ridge, they'll be here with the chopper. You'll be all right. I promise you."

Matt placed a soft kiss on each of her closed eyelids. "Dear God," he prayed aloud, "let her live."

He was reluctant to leave her for the time it would take to bring in help, but it had to be done. With a parting glance over his shoulder, Matt hastened down the trail. Time and surroundings became blurred in his haste and concern for Katy's life. He trotted where the terrain would allow it, and with the pounding of each step he repeated over and over to himself, "Please God, let her live. Please God, let her live."

His crisp directions over the radio when he reached the pickup belied the tremendous emotional involvement he felt in Katy's rescue.

He was still climbing on the return trip when he heard the chopper land in the meadow above him. He had asked for a large enough crew to carry Katy down off the ridge because the rescue vehicle would be unable to land closer than the meadow.

By the time Matt reached the clearing, the chopper crew was emerging from the trees with a stretcher bearing Katy's unconscious form.

"Drop off the crew at the station," Matt shouted to the pilot over the noise of the whirling blades. "I'll fly with her to Mount Lewis."

Katy lay in the same state of unawareness, somewhere between life and death, as she was loaded gently onto the helicopter.

Mount Lewis was forty minutes away by air. After depositing the extra crew members at the ranger station, Matt impatiently watched as the rounded, tree-covered mountains passed with agonizing slowness beneath them. There had never before seemed to be such an infinite maze of ridges lying south of the high plateau country where Mount Lewis was situated.

He was perspiring as he sat beside the stretcher with the unconscious girl, but at long last Mount Lewis came into view.

Having been forewarned by radio, the hospital staff was expecting her, and Katy was immediately admitted while Matt provided the admittance information.

She was wheeled off to a private room, and an hour passed before Matt was allowed to rejoin her.

"Mr. Moss," a starched nurse addressed him when he was at last allowed admittance to Katy's room, "can you give us names and phone numbers of Miss Ketchum's family? If not, her clothes are in that drawer." She pointed to an open drawer adjoining the closet door. "If you would like to go through them, perhaps you'll find the information we need."

Matt was more than happy to help. He tried to recall

the last name of Katy's fiancé. Then it came to him. She had had a letter from Richard in her pocket the first night he had seen her. She had been carrying it with her the day of the storm; it was there in her cut-offs' pocket. There was a return address on the envelope and Matt told the nurse he would notify her fiancé and get Katy's parents' names from him.

The receiver was slippery in his perspiring hand as Matt waited for the call to go through.

"Yes?" It was a woman's voice, Richard's mother.

Matt identified himself and obtained the number of the prosecuting attorney's office where her son could be reached.

His second attempt was successful and the secretary connected him with Richard.

"Richard Parks here," said an impatient voice.

"Mr. Parks, this is Matthew Moss. I'm a ranger with the forest service and I'm calling you from Mount Lewis."

"Yes, what is it?"

"I'm afraid I have some bad news for you. A friend of yours, Katy Ketchum, is in the hospital here in Mount Lewis."

"Oh, my God. Is she hurt?"

"She was trapped under a tree that fell in a thunderstorm. She was unconscious for three days before we found her and brought her off the mountain by helicopter."

"Damn girl. I told her not to go into the woods alone." The voice was anxious now. "Will she be okay?"

"We don't know yet. She's still unconscious, but she's getting good care and we should know something soon. I'll keep in touch. Her parents should be notified. Can you take care of that?"

"Sure, Moss, but do me a favor, would you? They'd probably like to hear from you since you're the guy who found her."

Richard gave Matt the Spokane name, address, and phone number of Katy's parents.

"I'm grateful for your finding her. I really wish I could get up there to be with her, but we've got a big case going to trial in the morning. I've put a lot of research into it and I'd sure hate to miss it. You understand. Look, if she's not out of the woods by the weekend, let me know and I'll fly up."

"Don't lose any sleep over it, Richard," Matt said with more sarcasm than he intended. "I'll keep in touch. In fact, if I can clear it with the station, I'll be staying here for a few days—as long as Katy needs me."

"As long as Katy needs you? So that's the way it is. I didn't think she had the guts to stick it out alone in the mountains."

Matt felt his head start to pound. "I think you're doing Katy a disservice, Richard. She's as brave and fine . . ."

"Okay, okay. I apologize. Anyway, let me know when she regains consciousness. I know you'll look after her in the meantime."

Matt could hardly believe the nonchalance of the man who had hung up so unconcernedly. If he were in Richard's place he'd be frantic with worry. How could Katy have experienced a loving relationship with such an unfeeling, jealous clod?

After calling Katy's parents and making arrangements to meet them at the hospital the next day, he returned to her room. He looked at the pale face framed by the starched whiteness of the bed, her dark hair spread across the pillow. He felt a surge of love for the infinitely sweet expression of her still face. He held her hand in his, but he longed to take her in his arms, to will her into consciousness, to tell her how strongly he felt about her.

Matt drew a chair alongside the bed and began his solitary vigil.

From his post outside the door, Matt could hear the sound of soft weeping within Katy's room. The door opened and a tall, slender woman with short black hair emerged.

"Oh, Matt," she said, "I can't control myself when I see my little girl lying in there as still as death."

"I'm sorry, Mrs. Ketchum. I wish there was more we could do. The doctors are keeping her body nourished with IV's, but we need to get in touch with her spirit, her will to live."

"In that case, she needs our prayers now, Matt. It's out of our hands. When I think what would have happened if you hadn't found her . . ."

Katy's father joined them in the hall. He was a large, ruddy-faced man with laugh lines deeply etched around his eyes, but that day his eyes were not laughing. Bert Ketchum looked at his wife, Jane, and shook his head sadly. "It's still touch and go, sweetheart."

"I know, Bert."

"Why don't you two get a cup of coffee while I sit with Katy?" Matt suggested.

They consented and headed for the coffeeshop while Matt resumed his vigil beside Katy's bed. Her skin had taken on a better color and her life signs were returning to normal; yet she was in what Dr. Langley had described as a deeply comatose state. When, or even if, she would awaken was, as Mrs. Ketchum had said, out of human hands.

The Ketchums spent two days at Katy's bedside before Jane Ketchum at last convinced her husband to return home. There was nothing more he could do in Mount Lewis. The doctors had refused to transfer Katy to Spokane. That they were possibly in for a long ordeal was a distinct possibility, and Jane was adamant about her husband returning to work. He would be close enough by air if he was needed in an emergency.

"Well, son," Bert Ketchum said later in parting, "you're a fine young man, and I'm grateful for what you've done for my Katy." He cleared his throat. "I'm not sure why it's necessary for you to stay on when they won't let her own father remain, but then maybe you and Katy know each other better than I thought."

Matt was embarrassed to have to justify his own continued presence. "I ran into Katy just a couple of times while she was camping in my district." He looked at Bert Ketchum as if weighing the wisdom of continuing, and decided to plunge ahead. "Mr. Ketchum, I feel that somewhere, sometime, Katy and I have known one another before." He passed a hand wearily across his eyes. "Maybe I'm just tired, talking like this." He laughed nervously.

"Go on," Bert said kindly.

"People scoff at the idea of having led past lives. I'm not sure of my own feelings regarding such things, yet I felt a tremendous attraction toward Katy the minute I saw her. It was more than attraction—it was complete understanding." His face reddened. "You probably think I'm some sort of crackpot."

"No, son, that you're not. Not by a long shot."

"Do you know," Matt continued, less apologetic, "I feel as though I know what is going on inside Katy's mind. Why, when I'm sitting beside her bed, sometimes I feel as if I could crawl inside her head and will her into consciousness.

"I feel as though I could almost experience the things that are going through her mind right now."

"Then, by God, son, you go right in there and get inside that girl's head. What you're talking about might not be reincarnation." He looked into Matt's worried brown eyes and said softly, "I think there's another word for what you're feeling for my little Katy and, son," he added, "you've got my blessing."

9

Takseen tugged on the reins of her mare and led the stumbling creature a few more paces upward on the muddy trail. No one rode that day on the treacherous slopes of the Lolo Trail as the Indians made their way up the steep, winding path. Some of the ponies found the trail impassable and were left behind, their sturdy legs hopelessly caught in tangled masses of downed timber and brush. They tossed their heads in fright and frustration, but their piteous neighing was nearly drowned in the pounding of the rain. The unseasonable rains had continued unabated since the people had begun their wilderness trek across the top of Idaho into the forbidding Bitterroot Mountains.

Three times Takseen heard shots ring out, but she couldn't see through the curtain of rain that blotted from view the weary train of Indians and pack animals. Suddenly there was a sliding, thrashing sound as a pony behind her mare fell to its knees on the trail. She looked back in time to see its helpless body slide over the edge of a rocky ravine. Buffalo Robe, traveling behind Takseen, left the trail and disappeared over the rock ledge. A few moments passed and there was a single rifle shot. Takseen wondered how many hapless creatures hadn't met such a merciful end. The Indians' passing was marked by dead and dying animals who could not negotiate the deep windfalls and steep washouts.

The Lolo Trail led upward through thickly forested slopes to a high ridge trail. From the ridge the mountains rolled off on all sides in a maze of wilderness. The river that rushed through the valley two thousand feet below was swollen with the mighty deluge, and its thundering descent over massive boulders could be heard from the ridge whenever the rains momentarily ceased their monotonous drumming.

The lodgepole pines grew thickly all across the summit, and although that route was the main trail to Montana and the buffalo country, it was ill defined after a severe winter. Downed trees, uprooted by winds, lay crisscrossed everywhere, densely matted together. Those windfalls slowed and sometimes halted the journey of the retreating Nez Perce. Rock slides and washouts further obliterated traces of the narrow trail that edged the cliffs. It was an arduous trip for the women and children and babies who crept perilously along the narrow ledges, shivering from the constant rains and the frost-bitten nights. The animals suffered doubly, for there was poor grazing atop the ridges, and dwarf lupine and wire grass had to suffice as a meager diet.

Takseen had ample time to reflect on the events of the past month, days filled with skirmishing, fighting, and negotiating, finally leading to the decision by the chiefs that the people would leave the Idaho country, move peaceably into Montana, and there join with their Crow brothers on the plains of Montana. Though the decision of the chiefs was unanimous, Takseen knew that Joseph's innermost desire was not to leave the Wallowa Valley permanently, but, through peaceable behavior, to be allowed to return one day.

Takseen felt in her heart that the goal of reaching the Montana plains was the only justification for the suffering endured by her people. For the rest, she was bitter and upset over the events of the past month. After the sweet taste of victory at Whitebird her people had spent days eluding the white soldiers, who closely pursued them. So adept had her people become at outmaneuvering the long knives that the young braves had dubbed General Howard "General Day after Tomorrow." Her people had crossed and recrossed the Salmon, leaving the soldiers days behind, infuriated at the ease with which the Indians effected the difficult crossings.

The event that lay heaviest in Takseen's heart was the Clearwater Battle. They had been camped on the south fork of the Clearwater at the base of a cliff when shells from Howard's cavalry started landing. Herdsmen drove horses up the ravines in a diversionary movement while the warriors encircled and held a strategic spring. Hopes of another Nez Perce victory were dashed when white reinforcements caused the Indians to flee, leaving much of what they owned on the banks of the Clearwater.

Generations of tribal treasures and possessions had fallen into the greedy hands of looters. Among them was a small glass ornament given to Gray Deer's grandmother seventy years earlier by the Lewis and Clark expedition. For Gray Deer, as for others, the gifts of those first white men had always symbolized the peace that had existed for generations between the whites and the Nez Perce; the loss of that single glass ornament had in turn symbolized the irreparable breach between the two civilizations. Since that time Gray Deer had been filled with despair, and Takseen was forced to become nearly a full-time mother to her infant sister.

The Clearwater battle was considered by some to be a defeat, marking the first Indian casualties. There was rumor that the whites claimed twenty-three dead, but Takseen knew

of only four. In addition to the deaths there were several
wounded. Of 450 noncombatants in the fight, it was ironic
that Pale Moon was among the few wounded.

Takseen's reflections were interrupted by a soft moaning
ahead. It was Pale Moon. Buffalo Robe had tied her astride
a strong pony when her high fever made walking impossible.
The arm wound she'd received from a stray bullet at the
battle of the Clearwater was infected and the resulting temperature left her delirious at times.

The moaning drew her attention and she looked at her
friend. As she looked, Pale Moon's pony stumbled, throwing
the girl against a tree and crushing the wounded arm against
the trunk. Pale Moon surely would have fallen had she not
been securely tied in the saddle.

Takseen rushed to her friend's side. The girl's round face
was deathly white and her eyes were bright with fever. Takseen raised Pale Moon upright in the saddle and picked up
the reins.

"I'll lead your pony for you, my friend. All will be well."
Pale Moon looked uncomprehendingly at Takseen with her
bright stare. "Put this blanket about your shoulders," Takseen
admonished her, removing the sodden blanket that hung
about Pale Moon's body. The covering she gave her in exchange was scarcely less wet. "Soon we'll be in the land of
the buffalo where the sun always shines. Then your fever
will dry up."

There was a faint answering smile as Takseen's words
penetrated Pale Moon's fever-racked body.

Takseen devoted her energies to Pale Moon the rest of
the day. The difficulty of the trail did not diminish; one
sharp-edged mountain followed another, so that after attain-
ing one ridge, the retreating Indians were forced down steep
switchbacks into the canyon depths, only to labor up succeed-
ing ridges. The pattern was repeated until the gray skies

parted late in the afternoon, revealing the sun for the first time. The weary bands of traveling Nez Perces erected hasty shelters. The lodgepoles had been left behind on the Clearwater camp, so their evening lodgings were makeshift.

It wasn't until Takseen had helped make Pale Moon as dry and comfortable as possible that she discovered the absence of Buffalo Robe. At first she thought little of it. He had surely gone into the timber in search of fresh meat.

The next morning Buffalo Robe still had not returned. The leaden skies again were unburdening themselves of vast quantities of rain, and Takseen felt a sensation of fear crawling within her stomach. Why had he not returned?

A hoarse whisper from Pale Moon interrupted her silent fears. "Water," she called softly.

It was the first intelligible word she had uttered in two days, and Takseen fervently hoped that Pale Moon was improving. She hurried to her friend's side, but the bright fever look of the eyes had not abated. Rain was dripping in rivulets down her cheeks and her body was wracked with shivers.

"Water," she whispered again.

Takseen held a drinking vessel to her cracked lips and was surprised to feel how thin Pale Moon's shoulders had become. She was normally a round-faced girl, but her cheekbones showed prominently through the flesh.

"You need some strong hot broth, my friend." There had been few cooking fires on the trail, so little time had been spent in food gathering. Meals were limited to roots and berries that could be gathered, or an occasional salmon. Even though there was little doubt that Howard's men were following a day or two behind, Takseen knew that a cooking fire and a bowl of hot broth might determine whether or not Pale Moon lived or died that day.

"We'll stay behind this morning. I will heat some broth

for you and dry your clothing over the fire." Pale Moon blinked in what Takseen hoped was an indication of comprehension. She conferred with Pale Moon's family and her own. In her insistence, Takseen got her way; Pale Moon's mother was desperately tired and was grateful for the help, and her own mother agreed to go on because she didn't have the strength to catch up should she fall a day's journey behind.

While Takseen labored over the damp wood, coaxing it into a small blaze, the sounds of her people striking camp came to her quietly against the continuous backdrop of falling rain. She sheltered her fire with an improvised lean-to and under it began to dry two blankets and some garments for Pale Moon.

The people began filing past, mounted on that particular stretch of trail, while their horses were fresh from a night's rest.

"Hssst." It was Broken Wing hissing at Takseen as she rode by. "Stir these into the broth," she said, tossing a packet of herbs to Takseen. "They will give her strength." Takseen accepted them gratefully.

"Don't tarry, daughter," Gray Deer advised from the saddle as she rode by. "The long knives may be close behind." Takseen longed to call out that Buffalo Robe was gone, that she could not leave until he'd returned, but she would only be burdening her mother with another worry, so she let it pass. "We will be with you by nightfall," she told her.

From her cradleboard on Gray Deer's back, Takseen's infant sister broke into a brief smile at the sight of her older sister. "If such a wet, undernourished child has a smile for me this day, I will set my worries aside," Takseen told herself firmly.

She knew that Joseph had sent five warriors to the rear

to guard the retreating line. Perhaps Buffalo Robe had joined them. Such a thought made it impossible not to worry. Perhaps the warriors were giving battle with the soldiers even then.

The morning wore on. Pale Moon had gratefully sipped the nourishing broth, and the feverish glint in her eyes had, after a time, begun to disappear. Occasionally she uttered a coherent word.

"Let me look at that arm," Takseen said, lifting the injured member and stripping the wet bandage from it. That time Pale Moon didn't wince when it was unwrapped, but there was fear in her eyes as she watched.

Then the tension fled from Takseen's face. "Hunyewat be praised. It doesn't appear so angry. Perhaps when your pony stumbled yesterday, the blow to your arm helped the poison to leave your wound. If we can keep you warm and dry now, your recovery will be certain."

There was an answering nod from Pale Moon and a faint smile appeared on her face. "I will get better," she affirmed. Her voice was still a whisper, but it had lost its hoarseness.

Takseen rewrapped the arm with a dry cloth and helped Pale Moon into the garments that at last had dried.

It was the middle of the afternoon and they could afford to delay their departure no longer.

"You look worried." Pale Moon had become almost talkative. "Don't be afraid for my sake. I'm weak, but much improved. Do you fear that the soldiers will catch up with us? Those 'walk-a-heaps.' " She laughed softly. "They are nothing but squaw soldiers." Some of her old confidence was returning. "They will be many days behind."

Takseen finally confided her source of worry to her friend. "Yes, those things are on my mind. Though I no longer fear for your life, nor am I frightened of the soldiers, I fear for the safety of my betrothed." She explained how Buffalo Robe had disappeared from the pack train.

"No wonder. I'd be worried too. But don't you think he'll soon return, perhaps with a nice fat rabbit or even a deer?"

"Perhaps. Come. We must leave now or we won't catch the others before nightfall."

Takseen boosted Pale Moon onto her horse and the two girls followed the trail, distinctly marked by the passing of the others.

Gray skies shaded into a moonless night. The rain ceased toward nightfall. The trail the girls had followed was fresh but fully as tortuous as the previous day's. They had traveled five hours without a rest when darkness finally forced them to a halt.

"We surely shall find the others before the sun is high tomorrow. We can go no farther tonight," Takseen admitted. She led the tired ponies to a clearing that offered some pasturage and staked them out. "Let's camp here beside the trail."

"But if the soldiers come?"

"We'll have no fire, and we'll be concealed in the trees. Don't worry."

The girls consumed a few handfuls of pemmican and dried berries. Takseen improvised a rough shelter of brush and blankets, but in no way could they find a spot for sleeping that was free from the penetrating dampness and incessant dripping from trees and bushes.

Pale Moon's head had cleared and her wound showed signs of healing. Yet she was weakened from the journey, and within minutes she gratefully slipped into a deep sleep.

Takseen was not so fortunate. Her thoughts were still with her betrothed. Nor had she forgotten the threat of soldiers to the rear.

She listened to the rustlings of the night creatures. Most

were small scampering sounds of nocturnal animals, but once a heavy trodding sounded nearby. Branches broke beneath the weight of an unseen creature stalking past the perimeter of the camp. Takseen had no fear of the large game animals who hunted those hills, with one exception; *hohots* the grizzly bear was a creature whose presence could freeze the blood of any Indian.

The stalker in the bushes moved on, and a clear descending call broke the stillness. It was the call of a screech owl, and it reassured Takseen. She touched the amulet close to her heart, symbol of her *wyakin*, recalling the victory celebration when Buffalo Robe had returned it to her. The cool stone had the effect of comforting her. "All will be well," she decided, and she too slept at last.

Takseen was uncertain how much time had passed when she became aware of horses approaching. Their gait was slow but steady, and the sounds of their neighing and blowing came to her from close by. The advance group seemed to be riderless, for she had not yet heard the sound of voices. The horses discovered the spring that had enticed Pale Moon and Takseen to camp at that spot, and they clustered about its water.

Pale Moon slept on. Takseen was alone with her fear. She heard voices then, low, quiet sounds, but indistinguishable. Were they Howard's men? She waited tensely. Her bravado fled as she recalled whispered tales of what could befall an Indian girl captured by white soldiers. The moments passed slowly and still there was no recognizable voice.

Then came the sound of laughter and a deep reply. Takseen had no doubts. She heard the voice of Buffalo Robe, returning with the warriors Joseph had sent to guard the entrance to the Lolo Trail.

Their mood was light. Surely that meant good news! The

girls' mounts answered the riderless horses from their concealed spot deep within the underbrush, and the sharp ears of Buffalo Robe heard the nickering welcome. The warriors drew abreast of the camp and Buffalo Robe called, "Who goes there?"

"Lay down your weapons. It is only I, Takseen, and my friend Pale Moon, who lies ill from a bullet wound." So saying, Takseen stepped into the clearing beside the trail. The sight of her betrothed, well and strong and safely returned, made her long to throw herself into his arms, but the reunion somehow seemed to require restraint. When would the time come that they could be together as man and wife? Tears of frustration rose in Takseen's eyes and she took a step toward him.

Buffalo Robe dismounted and she was in his arms. He pressed his cheek to hers. The other five warriors busied themselves with settling the horses and making camp, and in their discreet absence, Takseen and Buffalo Robe shared the events of the past day.

"I was frightened for your safety," she told him, silently urging him to tell what had happened, yet afraid he would think her interfering.

"Tell me first why you're here, little Willow."

Takseen explained about Pale Moon's fever and her recovery, assuring him that they were probably only a short distance from the main body of the camp. "And you, dear one?" she questioned.

"I was angered at the rout of the Clearwater. We were not whipped by those squaw soldiers. Why should we leave our possessions to those greedy white men? My heart was angry and I told myself, 'I will go back and make them sorry for what they did.' I was not afraid to die." His eyes softened.

"Except for you, little Willow. I would not want to die without first having you for my wife."

She laid her head lovingly on his shoulder and he held her close while he finished his tale.

"I joined the five warriors Joseph had selected to guard the entrance to the trail. They had made a clever trap; in two places on the trail they sawed tree trunks nearly through but left them standing upright. When Howard's men passed between the severed trees, the trunks would topple, trapping the soldiers in a narrow passage, a good plan—if it had worked. A small party of white soldiers did pass through, intending to harry our rear, but their horses smelled our ponies. In their fear they pawed the ground and the riders discovered sawdust in the underbrush. They sensed our trap, but we stopped them anyway. Firing at them we killed one of their scouts and wounded two others." Buffalo Robe laughed. "They ran home like whipped dogs with tails between their legs. We rounded up a fine herd of horses that we'd left behind on the Clearwater. That's why your mare made such happy sounds from her hiding place. She knew her friends were back!"

It was a cause for happiness, to pay back the white man in some small way. Takseen felt warm and happy and secure in Buffalo Robe's arms, and she hated to part from him. In her mind she was weighing her words carefully, torn with desire and frustration, as they stood together in the vast dripping forest.

"My husband to be, these times are uncertain. The days are long. The nights are cold. If it is your wish, I could make your bed warm this night."

Buffalo Robe laid a restraining finger on her lips. "Little Willow, that is my deepest desire, but in wartime, a man does not sleep with a woman. It is forbidden."

Takseen felt her cheeks growing hot in the darkness. "I meant no harm," she whispered.

"Of course you didn't, but I mustn't tempt the evil spirits to rob me of my *wyakin*. I shall need a strong guardian spirit in the days to come."

He gave her a parting hug and wiped a tear from her cheek. "It is settled, then. We must be patient yet a little longer."

10

The Lolo Trail demanded seven more arduous days of trekking. Though the journey was difficult, it took no toll of human life.

Takseen saw little of Buffalo Robe, for he had left with a party of warriors to travel back to Kamiah. Their instructions were to burn dwellings in the settlement and generally cause confusion so that General Howard would think the retreating Indians were returning westward. Hopefully the diversion would delay General "Day After Tomorrow" even further.

On the afternoon of the seventh day the travelers arrived at Nasook Nema, Salmon Creek. It lay high in the mountains at the western end of the Lolo Trail where a narrow pass led into Montana.

There was fresh meat that night in the cooking pot. Lone Coyote had brought down two deer, sharing them with other families who had not fared so well in hunting. A cooking fire was allowed that evening in recognition of the general sense of safety and well-being the Indians were beginning to feel. Surely they would leave the war behind in Idaho!

Unfortunately, the sense of well-being was premature; toward evening a warrior from the forward scouting party came riding into camp. "Soldiers in front of us! Building a fort. They are heading us off."

The announcement brought a startled reawakening to those, like Takseen, who were enjoying a hot meal and a sense of peace for the first time in many days.

They completed their meal in a state of anxiety while the chiefs went off to hold council with the leaders of the soldiers.

The peace talks took place within view of the camp in an open meadow out of rifle range. Takseen watched anxiously, trying to make sense from the quiet gesturing of Joseph and the others. Apparently there was little to agree upon, for the chiefs' delegation returned shortly.

Joseph was angry when he returned. "They want what we will not give them," he announced. "If we wish to enter the valley, they say we must give up all our horses and stock, surrender all our arms. I for one will not walk unarmed and unmounted through the Bitterroot Valley." He set his face sternly. "They have placed a log barricade across a narrow place in the valley. We shall not be stopped by a pile of logs! Instead, we will go around them, high above on the ledges. We will find another way."

"Why not fight them?" Hohots demanded. "How many soldiers are there?"

"Thirty soldiers. Maybe a hundred volunteers. Also a handful of Flathead scouts." Joseph spat in disgust at the treachery of the Indians who had formerly been their friends. "The Flatheads are wearing white cloths on their arms and heads, so they will not shoot each other."

Hohots laughed at the image Joseph suggested.

"You ask why we do not meet them head on and fight," Joseph continued. "I shall tell you. A hundred of them are not worth a hair on the head of one of my brave fighting men."

Joseph looked at the gathering crowd about him and a

smile twitched at the corners of his mouth. It was the first time the Wallamwatkins had seen any sign of mirth on Joseph's somber features for longer than they could remember, and their hearts were lightened.

"Let us go around them, to the top of the mountain. Then they will see themselves for the foolish dogs they are," he concluded.

There was laughter at the thought of rendering the soldiers and their log barricade impotent. Early the next morning the people began moving. Unwilling to wait for a noon appointment to continue the parley, they began the upward climb through a northward inclined ravine. To wait would only have meant allowing more time for reinforcements to appear at Captain Rawn's improvised fort.

In a bold tactical move, Joseph moved all the families and their possessions up the dizzying heights along narrow ledges that were normally followed only by mountain goats.

High above the log barricade, Takseen looked down on the fortification. The citizen volunteers had all left, apparently trusting the word of the chiefs that they wished to pass through Montana peacefully. The small number of bluecoats and the handful of scouts, whose white headbands identified them clearly from that distance, seemed a pitiful token force against the audacious flanking movement of the Nez Perce.

So ridiculous did the soldiers' position seem that the Indians spontaneously broke into song. From several hundred throats came a chanting, haunting melody as they wended their way along dizzying ledges. The astonished soldiers could only stare dumbly upward.

There was a lighthearted sense of joy in camp that night. It was the first night in Montana, and again the people dared to hope they had left the war behind them in Idaho. Their flanking movement had surprised Captain Rawn and his party

so much that no attempts had been made to follow the retreating Indians.

Lest the mood get too lighthearted, Joseph spoke to his
people that night. "You have the right to be happy tonight.
We refused to surrender to the bluecoats who told us, 'You
cannot get by us.' We answered them, 'We are going by
you without fighting if you will let us, but we are going by you
anyhow.' " There was a twittering among the listeners, but
Joseph held up a hand and quieted them.

"Remember, we made a treaty with those soldiers. We
said we would pass through the Bitterroot country peacefully.
If we need provisions we will trade for them or buy them outright. We will go peaceably to the buffalo country."

"And there will be no more war," came the tired voice of
an old crone.

"No one can promise that, old woman," Joseph answered
sadly.

The sun shone brightly in Montana, and as Takseen
had promised Pale Moon, its healing rays dried up her wound
and her strength returned. The sun proved a balm to all the
others as well as to Pale Moon. Together they had spent
many grueling days on the treacherous pathways of the Lolo
Trail.

There was further good news. The war party returned
intact from Kamiah. Takseen was joyful at Buffalo Robe's
safe return.

The pace through the Bitterroot country was leisurely,
and they covered no more than twelve miles a day. There was
time for cattle and horses to graze on the lush pasturage and
to recover the strength they had lost on the long trip when
there was little to eat.

"The war is over. Hunyewat be praised. The war is over."
That was the sentiment expressed repeatedly by the people

on the trail who encountered no trouble in the Bitterroot Valley.

Takseen was not as complacent as some of the other young people, but even she began to relax as she saw the peaceful exchanges between her people and the Montana whites. At the settlements they traded for flour and sugar, coffee and tobacco, paying for their purchases with gold dust and currency.

Only one small incident upset the orderliness of their passing. A handful of Toohoohoolzote's more unruly braves entered the ranch of Myron Lockwood, helping themselves to staples, tools, and clothing. Looking Glass was highly angered by their behavior, and he forced the young men to put Lockwood's brand on seven of their own horses and place them in the white rancher's pasture.

Even the choice of a route was a sign of their peaceful intentions. They could have chosen one of several routes into the buffalo country to the east. Their decision had been to travel south down the Bitterroot Valley and over the continental divide, into the Big Hole Basin. This alternative was by far the longest, many days longer than the other, more direct routes, but the Indians had word that their way was blocked to the north by soldiers, and to the east lay Fort Missoula and Fort Shaw. Therefore, by avoiding the white soldiers, the Nez Perce hoped to prove their peaceful intentions.

The bands of Nez Perce, refreshed by the welcome relief of the pleasant Bitterroot Valley, arrived after several days at their old camp below Ross Hole. That camp had special significance because of the Medicine Tree nearby, a traditional spot of peace and neutrality.

It was the next morning that Lone Bird announced the disturbing contents of his dream of the previous night. The sun had just risen when he rode through camp shouting, "My shaking heart tells me trouble and death will overtake us if we make no hurry through this land! I cannot smother, I cannot hide what I see. I must speak what is revealed to me. Let us be gone to the buffalo country!"

Then Wahlitits, one of Joseph's warriors, came forward, telling of his own dream, which he had not dared reveal before that time. "I had a vision," he told the people as they clustered about their lodge doors, "a vision that soon I would die in battle. That soon only a handful of our people would be living." Wahlitits wife, large with child, looked at him fearfully at this revelation.

Instead of general fear at the forecast of doom, the rest of the people scoffed at the prophecies. The chiefs set no particular significance to them and didn't change their plans to journey two more days, then rest in the Big Hole Basin. From their demeanor there was little to indicate that that journey was any different from former trips to the buffalo country.

Takseen grudgingly accepted the attitude of the chiefs. Buffalo Robe, taking advantage of their complacency, approached Takseen at the Ross Hole Camp.

Darkness had fallen, and she was extinguishing the small cooking fire that burned before the tepee. Her family was within, preparing for sleep.

"Little Willow," Buffalo Robe called softly.

Takseen looked up into his handsome face. More than ever she longed for the day when she would be his wife.

"Is your father within?" he inquired.

Takseen nodded and announced his presence through the open door.

Yellow Moccasin rushed out eagerly to behold the warrior who had given him his wonderful horse, Spotted Eagle. He too was eager to have Buffalo Robe as a member of the family.

Gray Deer joined them and invited Buffalo Robe to come and sit before the small fire within the tepee.

They talked of the weather and of the events of the past few days. Takseen waited impatiently to hear the real reason for his call.

"Honored parents," Buffalo Robe addressed Takseen's elders respectfully, "I have come seeking your advice." Lone Coyote, squatting on his heels, nodded encouragement.

"I will bare to you what is in my heart. I have long desired to make your daughter my wife, yet my path is blocked by the events that have occurred." Buffalo Robe continued in the somewhat stilted fashion he used when addressing Takseen's parents. "Would you, in your wisdom, give permission for our marriage to take place during this journey? The times are not as they once were. Perhaps the usual customs could not all be observed. Yet because the chiefs feel there is little threat to us at this time, surely our marriage could take place, almost as it would had there been no war."

His last statement was actually a question as he sought permission from the old man.

Lone Coyote sat in silence for several moments, watching the smoke that coiled toward the smokehole above him. Then he spoke.

"We are not at war today. Yet we have no guarantee of peace for tomorrow. It seems a foolish time to marry." Takseen felt her hopes drop. Her father looked so stern. Then he continued, and a slight smile creased his face. "Yet I too was young once."

Lone Coyote looked at his daughter, her black eyes reflecting the flames as he gazed at her across the fire. "I know the frustration in your hearts from the long delay. Because I understand these things, because I love my daughter, even though these times are uncertain, I will grant my permission."

Takseen smiled happily at her father, pleased and a little surprised at his perception of her feelings.

"When we reach the Big Hole Basin your marriage may be completed. We will be there several days—almost enough time to observe the customs and do it correctly."

Buffalo Robe rose to leave, but Lone Coyote stopped him. "I think this is a matter for Joseph to decide also. If he agrees, then all will be as I have said."

By the following evening, at the camp on Trail Creek, Takseen had been assured that permission was granted. Her heart sang as she began to prepare in two days what a bride under normal circumstances would spend months preparing. First there was a bridal dress to complete. From a soft piece of deerskin, Takseen and Gray Deer and Broken Wing worked far into the night fashioning a dress. Their willing hands decorated the bodice with beads and quillwork and trimmed the neck in rabbit fur. It was softly fringed at the bottom, and when completed, the dress was lovely.

The two days' journey to the camp along the Big Hole River passed in a blur for Takseen, so deliriously happy was she in her preparations. Within two days she would be the wife of the warrior Buffalo Robe.

11

"There will be lodgepoles enough here," Takseen observed over her shoulder to her mother as they rode across the long alpine meadow that marked Iskumtselalik Pah, the Place of the Ground Squirrels. That was the Big Hole Basin, the traditional neutral camping place of many tribes. Across the banks of the gently winding Big Hole River, beyond the thick growth of willows that bordered it, were the pine forests of the mountains slopes.

Looking across the valley, lush with sagebrush and flowers, Gray Deer eyed the pine forest and agreed with her daughter. "At last there will be time to cut and dry the lodgepoles which we will take to the buffalo country." Makeshift poles, hastily cut on the Lolo Trail, had never been allowed to season and were only a temporary measure.

They established their camp on the banks of the Big Hole River. Since the people anticipated a stay of several days, they took care in setting up the village. The eighty-nine lodges were arranged in a V-shape with a partly open court in the middle. The erection of the tepees consumed the remaining daylight hours, but during that time the men had time to fish and hunt, providing fresh food for the more than six hundred people.

Takseen had many relatives, and they all gladly shared in the wedding preparations. The wedding was to take place on the evening of the second full day in Iskumtselalik Pah. Some friends aided in the household chores of setting up camp and food preparation, while others joined in gathering sufficient household goods for Takseen to establish housekeeping in her own lodge.

There were many volunteers, because that celebration, hasty though it was, was the first in many moons; a spirit of anticipation swept the family and friends.

On the first morning the sun quickly dissipated the mists from the river, revealing a beautiful day. Time passed quickly in a flurry of work and excitement for Takseen.

"You wait here," Pale Moon ordered her late in the afternoon. The group of giggling girls surrounding Takseen pushed her down beside a pile of robes and blankets and household goods they had accumulated. While she watched, the girls dashed off, each one carrying several items from the pile. Root baskets, dried meat, bark dishes, horn spoons, prized kettles, pots and pans, all generously donated from family and friends, disappeared before her eyes as the girls raced with them across the camp.

At the far end of the village Buffalo Robe had been busy establishing a lodge to which he would take Takseen as his wife on the following night. From where she was seated, Takseen could not observe his efforts, nor was she supposed to. He and all the eager assistants were apparently contriving a surprise for her.

The girls soon returned, still smiling and laughing. They surrounded Takseen and, holding her by the arms, marched her in the direction of the new tepee.

"You must come with us now," Pale Moon told her. She wagged her finger at her friend. "Oh, you will be happy to see this."

"But not as happy as she'll be tomorrow night," a second girl giggled behind her hand.

Takseen had endured much of that good-natured teasing in the last two days. Her friends were envious at her winning such a handsome bridegroom, but their teasing was all in fun.

The wedding lodge was situated beside the banks of the stream where it bent to the southwest. The door faced the river, and the girls pushed Takseen through it, squeezing in beside her, until they all stood within the lodge.

"How beautiful!" Takseen exclaimed in delight as she surveyed the work of her friends. There within the lodge was everything she would need when she became Buffalo Robe's wife.

In one corner a pile of robes was stacked on the rush matting on the floor. There were more warm robes and soft skins for a bed. In various corners of the tepee, each in its own place, were the items she'd need for cooking—a stone mortar and pestle, dishes and utensils, and several baskets filled with roots. There was dried meat hanging from the top of the lodge, and a small fire was laid in the center beneath the smoke hole.

In another corner were the hunting and fishing weapons that belonged to Buffalo Robe.

Then the girls stepped aside, allowing Buffalo Robe to enter. As if they felt their presence an invasion of the privacy of the almost wedded pair, the girls silently slipped away.

The two, alone in the lodge they were soon to share, looked long into one another's eyes.

"This is all so hard to believe," Takseen breathed, gesturing to the collection of household items that surrounded them. "How generous everyone has been."

"They too are glad to share our happiness, little Willow, for we have all suffered hardships in the past few moons."

Two moons had passed since the crossing of the Snake, and Takseen thought back over those toilsome days, over the loss of life and property her people had endured; but mostly she thought of the loss of their homeland and her eyes grew large with tears.

Buffalo Robe brushed them away. "This is a time for happiness, little one," he told her. "Not tears."

"You're right," she said softly. "This place is beautiful, and we're safe at last. Yet my heart is sick for a glimpse of the valley of the Winding Water. Will we ever see it again?"

"Perhaps," he nodded, a faraway look in his eyes too.

Then he held her close, saying nothing, while the mixed feelings of joy and homesickness fought within her. She sobbed quietly for only a moment, and then her shaking shoulders stilled. She became aware of the strength and closeness of her betrothed.

"Tomorrow I will call you husband," she said, using the word shyly.

Buffalo Robe smiled into her black eyes. "These things," he gestured to all the corners of the tepee, "are they not an omen of the good life to come? We will have a long and happy life together, little Willow."

There was much merrymaking in camp that night. Takseen and her family, hard at work within their tepee, listened to the sounds of laughter and dancing as the young people paraded through camp. There was a general sense of well-being in that resting place, the Big Hole Valley.

"Why is Yellow Moccasin not yet back?" Gray Deer wondered aloud when the festivities outside had quieted down.

"He is probably with the boys playing the bone game. I saw him heading toward the river with his friends earlier."

Gray Deer shook her head in silent disapproval. Takseen knew her mother didn't care for the gambling game the boys played, even though they only played with sticks and bones.

It was getting late and Lone Coyote retired, leaving Gray Deer and Takseen to complete their sewing tasks. His part in the wedding would be to distribute gifts to the wedding guests, and having already made his plans accordingly, he soon joined his infant daughter in slumber.

"It's unfortunate," Takseen told her mother, who, not satisfied with the wedding dress, was adding an intricate pattern of colored beads across its bodice, "that Broken Wing cannot join us tomorrow in the celebration."

"She will be disappointed too, but she has gone where she is needed."

The old woman had been summoned by Sun Tied shortly after the evening meal to aid his wife in childbirth. Secluded in the hospital tent with the laboring young woman, Broken Wing would miss the festivities she so dearly loved.

"Look, Mother, at this gift she gave me before she left."

Gray Deer took the old medicine bag Takseen handed her.

"Did she tell you what it was for?"

"Yes, it contains the roots she uses to kill the pains of childbirth." Gray Deer handed them back and smiled knowingly.

"But, Mother," Takseen continued, "she said something strange. She told me, 'Little Willow, I won't be here to help you next year when you need these. By this time next year you will doubtless bear your husband a strapping son.' Then she not only gave me the roots, but she told me their identity and how to prepare them."

"That isn't so strange," Gray Deer said, holding her work closer in the diminishing firelight. "All old people think they will die. She told you her secret because she loves you."

Gray Deer stood and held up the dress for Takseen to examine. "It is finished."

"How beautiful!" Takseen exclaimed as she beheld the white doeskin dress with its trimmings of fringe and rabbit fur, quillwork and beading.

Then Gray Deer handed her two strips of rabbit fur and a purple scarf. "This fur you may use to tie your braids. Perhaps you will wish to use the scarf also."

"Thank you, Mother," Takseen said gratefully. "You have been so good."

"You are a worthy daughter. Come, let us put our work away. I think I hear Yellow Moccasin returning, and we must all get some sleep. Tomorrow is an imporant day."

Takseen slept restlessly in anticipation of her wedding day. It was not yet dawn when she rose from her bed of skins and silently picked up the wedding dress.

She slipped it over her head, enjoying the sensation of wearing something so lovely. Never had she had a dress like it.

All was still dark within the lodge and she stepped outside. The crisp air felt good, and the darkness quieted her anxious thoughts. "Perhaps a walk will calm my heart," she thought, and walked toward the far edge of camp, her steps automatically taking the direction to her bridal lodge.

The mists swirled thickly near the stream. Her steps led past the hospital lodge and she heard soft voices within. Then the air was punctuated by the cry of a newborn. Broken Wing had again succeeded in helping bring a new life into the world. Takseen's heart rejoiced at the miracle of birth, and she recalled her experience in witnessing it at Tepahlewam.

Only the birds and one lone herdsman were stirring at

that hour. With the awakening of the birds came the faintest tinge of pink in the east, a barely perceptible lifting of the darkness, but the mists continued to swirl. She could hear the herdsman as he made his way on horseback away from camp to the meadow where the ponies were kept.

Takseen was savoring that solitary moment on her wedding day when a shot rang out. Though she could not see, she sensed that the rider had fallen from his horse.

Before she had time to become alarmed, Takseen heard the sound she had come to dread. With no preliminaries, rifle fire began pattering into tepees, with a sound like rain, but far more deadly. A barrage of shots slammed into camp, spraying with mindless accuracy from the fearsome Gatling guns. Takseen stood in bewilderment for a moment, determined to rush back to her tepee, but trying to discover where the shots were coming from. Then she saw the rifle flashes. The soldiers were close by, secluded in the willows on the far bank of the stream.

Her white dress was a good target as she raced through the faint light. There were angry, surprised cries as the sleeping camp awoke to the predawn attack. She clutched the amulet at her breast, praying to her guardian spirit for protection for herself and all her dear ones.

"I am hit. I am killed," she heard an old woman cry out. Half-clad people were running everywhere, warriors trying to locate weapons, and women and children fleeing for the willows on the riverbank. In their blind haste they fled into the path of the fire. Those who made it took refuge in the willows while leaves and branches splintered about them, falling like rain from the continuous barrage of gunfire.

In the half-light, Takseen succeeded in crossing the camp without injury. Only a few paces from her lodge, she saw her father dash past, rifle in hand, wearing only a loincloth.

Then brave young Yellow Moccasin ran by, leading Buffalo Robe's horse War Bonnet. Behind her she heard the warrior shouting to both of them.

"Keep down!" he ordered. "Head for the water!" She could barely hear Buffalo Robe over the shouting and wailing and gunfire. The soldiers were plunging across the shallow river, intent then on carrying their attack into camp. She saw her father engaged in hand-to-hand combat; then he was lost to view as Buffalo Robe roughly shoved her to the ground. A shot sang past her ear; she had been its target, but it lodged instead in the plunging body of War Bonnet. The horse fell heavily to the ground, pinning Yellow Moccasin beneath him.

There were two soldiers running toward them, firing rapidly. Buffalo Robe dropped one of them, then engaged the other with his *kopluts*, his war club.

"To the river," he shouted to Takseen again through the din.

"Yellow Moccasin!" she shouted, but her voice was drowned in the dreadful sounds of battle. She tugged at the boy who was pinned beneath the horse. He cried out in anguish as she pulled with sudden strength, releasing his injured leg. It was mangled, but she had no time to assess his injuries. She clasped him under the arms and dragged him across the clearing.

By that time she realized her own lodge was empty. The whereabouts and the safety of her mother and baby sister were in the hands of the guardian spirits, and she whispered a silent prayer for their well-being.

The short distance to the river bank seemed an eternity as shots continued to fall. Cries of the wounded filled the air, but there was an added sound. The startled exclamations of the surprised people had turned to anger, and the warriors were rallying. Their war cries sent courage into the beleaguered noncombatants, and all those who could joined the fight.

Takseen somehow managed to drag her brother across the stream and push him into the shelter of the willows. The soldiers had all crossed to the camp side, but they trained their fire indiscriminately on camp and willow shelter both. A group of women and children lay in the bushes besides them when a soldier appeared, aiming his rifle point-blank at them.

"Stop, we are only women and children!" Takseen cried, stepping forward, speaking simultaneously with her hands.

The soldier's finger wavered on the trigger before an officer pushed the rifle barrel down, deflecting the shot.

It was light enough to see, but the scene before Takseen was so terrible she could scarcely take it all in. The sights she saw sickened her.

Across the way she saw the warrior Wahlitits firing from behind a log that lay in front of his tepee. In the next moment he was hit, and his wife, who appeared to be wounded, picked up his rifle and shot the soldier who had killed him. Then she too was struck, falling across the body of her husband. Takseen's heart was sick, for the wife of Wahlitits was soon to be a mother and had been her friend.

A boy of thirteen leaped across the river and took refuge nearby. "Jump across!" he urged a small brother who plunged after him. Only moments passed before the older boy lay dead, killed by a stray bullet. He lay half in the water while his younger brother started wailing. Takseen heard him whimper, "Where is my blanket?"

Before she could stop him, the small child was splashing across and running up the opposite bank to retrieve the blanket he had dropped. When he returned safely to the shelter he was still crying. Unable to comprehend the scope of destruction, the little boy cried, "Why is my brother sleeping so? In the camp there are many like him. All sleeping."

Takseen was moved to tears and could not answer. Then

she saw a further sight that filled her with agony. Only a hundred paces away her mother lay unmoving upon the ground. Her infant sister, lying on her mother's breast, cried piteously, waving a bloody arm up and down. The arm had been shattered and her hand, hanging only by a piece of flesh, dropped back and forth with the moving arm.

"Will anyone be spared?" Takseen thought as she witnessed the horrible sight. Except for the sake of Buffalo Robe, she would have gone willingly to her death.

Then a new dimension of agony was added as she watched the soldiers set fire to the tepees. "Surely there are little children sleeping within," she thought; to the smoke and flames were added the sounds of panic of those, mostly children, who had not already fled from their lodges.

The soldiers became confident of their victory, and they triumphantly carried their torches from one tepee to the next. Still, the Indians were not beaten; through the pall of smoke, the soldiers were unaware of the rally taking place. There was no really organized attack, but from the brush, from the creek bank, from the open prairie, from the hills, came a concerted rifle attack. The warrior's accuracy soon made the soldiers' position untenable. They were forced to retreat to a timbered area on a point of land above the camp, on the far side of the river.

The warriors held them there for the rest of the day, reversing the massacre into a siege that took a costly toll of soldiers' lives. While the Indian sharpshooters harried the soldiers, keeping them from wreaking further destruction on the innocents in camp, the surviving women and children, the old people, returned to the ruins to take stock of their losses, vainly hoping to find their loved ones alive amidst the smoking debris.

The destruction that greeted their eyes was horrifying. Amidst the smoke and the cries of the wounded arose a horrible lamentation from the grief-stricken surviviors. Their screams and cries echoed against the hills with an anguish that must have sent chills through the besieged attackers who lay defensively in hastily dug trenches.

There was no way to shut out the sights and sounds and the smell of death. Takseen carried her wounded brother into camp, but there was no one to help her with her burden. Elsewhere the survivors were gathering together the dead and wounded of their immediate families, but the loss of Takseen's family appeared total, and there were none to help her.

She found a pile of robes and laid her brother on them but could do nothing further for him until she had staunched the flow of blood from her infant sister's shattered arm. The baby's crying continued, but Takseen could not stop the spurting blood from flowing. Desperately, she carried the infant to the river and plunged the tiny arm into the water, but the icy stream did not help, and the child's cries grew weaker. The loss of blood soon took effect on the small body, and in a short time the baby's eyes glazed over in merciful death.

Now two lay dead before the smoking remains of the tepee, Gray Deer and her infant daughter. Takseen had not seen her father, old Lone Coyote, or Buffalo Robe since the shooting had begun. Nor had she seen Broken Wing. The thought of the hospital lodge and its helpless occupants filled her with alarm. She remembered Broken Wing's cryptic remark of the night before. She made her way past clusters of mourners, all occupied with treating their wounded and burying the dead, until she came to the hospital lodge. It stood alone, unharmed by fire, but when she looked in, another pitiful scene greeted her eyes. Broken Wing and the wife of Sun Tied lay dead on the floor, both shot through the head. The newborn lay in his mother's arms, his tiny head crushed

by a boot heel or a rifle butt. Takseen shut her eyes to the
sight; she felt she could witness no more suffering that day.
There were large tears in her eyes as she turned silently from
the lodge, closing the flap behind her. Head down and
shoulders bowed, she walked with slow steps to her own
smoldering lodge and collapsed in grief beside the body of her
mother.

At last she gave vent to her sorrow in loud, wailing sobs,
and that was the way Lone Coyote, himself bearing a shoulder
wound, found her when he rode into camp. He was leading
a horse with the body of Buffalo Robe flung across its back.

"Daughter," Lone Coyote called her softly.

Takseen looked up. Her father said nothing, but the tears
ran fast from his eyes and his heart was too sick to let him
speak. Takseen looked numbly at the body of her betrothed
and she stood, still wearing the dress that she was to have
been married in that day. It was stained with blood and dirt
and ashes, and she was suddenly aware of it and of the
terrible irony it represented.

Even in her grief, she knew her father's loss was just as
great. She stepped up to him, helping him dismount, and
together they stood, arm in arm, and wept, for the mother
and child that lay on the grass and for the dead warrior.

"The earth mother has claimed them," Lone Coyote said
softly. The blood that mingled with the earth and the grass
was drying, and Lone Coyote stoically set his face as he
began the grim task of burying his dead. His shoulder wound
was deep, but he worked heedless of the pain, and Takseen
helped him wordlessly.

Their ears were deaf to the desultory firing that continued,
just as they paid no heed to the instructions of Joseph as he
rode through camp urging haste in packing up the pitiful remnants of their possessions, haste in burying the dead. The

survivors must leave while the warriors remained behind to hold off the attackers, he told them.

Lone Coyote dug a shallow grave halfway up a ravine and there he carried the bodies one by one, tenderly laying his wife and baby daughter within the mother earth. Just as reverently he laid the body of Broken Wing beside them. She had been the bride of his youth, and though he had taken a second wife, he loved that one who had grown frail and old before her time. She had been childless, but she had generously lent her midwifery skills to all who had need of them.

He returned for the last body, but Takseen would not allow her father to remove Buffalo Robe just then.

"Just a moment longer, Father," she urged him tearfully. Takseen was washing the dirt from the warrior's face and the blood from his chest. His handsome face was peaceful in death, as though he were only sleeping. When she was done, she covered the fatal wound with a soft leather shirt. Like her dress, it was white, fringed at the bottom and trimmed in porcupine quills.

"This was to have been my wedding gift to you," she breathed softly into his unhearing ears. "Beloved," she whispered, and she laid her cheek against his for one last time.

"Let us take him now." She stood up and did not look again at the face of her betrothed.

"Why are you doing that?" Takseen asked her father when they had completed the burials.

Lone Coyote had dug up a sapling and was replanting it on the fresh graves. "We must conceal this spot, or the Bannock scouts who fought with the white soldiers will desecrate these graves. They will mutilate our dead." He placed rocks and leaves atop the loose earth around the young tree and soon there was no sign that the earth mother had reclaimed four of her children.

There was no room inside her heart for more sorrow, only an aching emptiness, and Takseen could later barely remember how she gathered their few remaining belongings, and with her wounded father and crippled brother, joined the pitiful line of Indians who straggled in groups from the Big Hole Valley.

12

The girl in the hospital bed lay exactly as she had for the past week, deathly still. Only the lifelines taped to her veins indicated that she still lived.

Matthew Moss was sitting alone at Katy's bedside, relieving Jane Ketchum of the vigil the two had kept continuously for more than a week.

Matt looked hard at the sleeping face, willing her with all his powers of concentration to awaken. "Please God, restore this girl to health," he prayed as he had done countless times before.

On that bright July morning, after a week of watching Katy lying there with no change in her condition, Matt saw a quiet stirring. Katy's head turned from side to side and her eyes flickered open. She looked at him, but he had the strange sensation that she was not focusing on him but on some other, or some memory locked in her subconscious.

Her lips moved and she stared at Matthew, but there was

no sound. He leaned across the bed, his ear beside her lips and she whispered again, "Beloved."

Matthew was puzzled. The endearment was clearly not meant for him, for in her present condition, Katy would have no recollection of Matt or of the circumstances which had put her in the hospital.

"Is it Richard you want?" Matt questioned softly, despising the name, but knowing he must be fair to Katy. After spending a day in Richard's company, Matt liked him even less than before, but he had to grudgingly admit that a girl might find Richard attractive. Smooth was probably a better word. Matt couldn't help but contrast his own lack of polish and his blunt manner of speaking with Richard's "charm." "What a hypocrite," Matt thought to himself.

Katy's blue eyes flickered again and opened wide. She shook her head "no" to his question about Richard and for one instant seemed to recognize Matt. With a look of utter sadness, she whispered the name, "Buffalo Robe," then wonderingly, "Matt?"

Matt took advantage of her seeming return to lucidity to explain what had befallen her.

"A storm? A fallen tree?" she queried as she tried to sort out the information he was giving her. Then she began to put the pieces together. "The journals! On top of the ridge!"

"Where, Katy?"

"Under the ledge. Just before the tree fell . . ."

"You said 'journals.' You must have found Grandpa John's second journal!"

Then the haze again clouded her eyes, and Katy lapsed into a semiconscious state. She rallied only one more time and staring hard at Matthew, she begged him, "You must find the journals. They are my salvation."

Matthew was puzzled by the coherence and intensity of her request and by the strangeness of it, but he understood the importance of retrieving the journals before they were damaged by exposure.

He clasped Katy's hand tightly. Her eyes were closed again and he was uncertain if she was still aware of his presence.

"I'll bring them to you," he promised and placed a kiss on her cool forehead.

To ask for yet another week's leave of absence was jeopardizing his job, but Matt requested it and was grudgingly granted the time.

Jane Ketchum would continue her watch at Katy's bedside, and she promised to keep in close touch with the Moose Meadow ranger station while he was gone. With luck, Matt's mission would take only a day and a half.

Without transportation in Mount Lewis, Matt was forced to hitchhike. He caught a ride that took him within fifteen miles of his headquarters, to the small logging town of Pinewood. From there he called in for a ride and his assistant, Rusty, delivered him an hour later at the station.

It was late in the afternoon, so Matt again tossed his rucksack into the pickup. He planned to spend the night at the fire tower.

Leaving the forest-service vehicle at the junction with Moose Meadow trail, he recovered the route that had by then grown very familiar. Matt noted that the forest had again dried out, probably having received no more rain since the big storm. That meant possible trouble for his district, but it was good news as far as the journals were concerned; they wouldn't have been disturbed by rain.

Less than two hours later Matt arrived atop the ridge.

Sitting in a hospital room for more than a week had left him slightly out of shape, and he had been breathing hard as he made his way up the final incline.

Nothing appeared changed at the site of the accident except for the absence of the little brown owl.

The tin box was not difficult to find, and a little distance away was the notepad in which Katy had begun to recopy the contents of the second journal. Katy's transcription had suffered from the storm and the pages were partially matted together, but Matt placed it in the tin box with the others.

There was almost time to return to headquarters, but he decided to hike on up to the fire tower. It was unmanned because of the help shortage, and he could be alone to spend the evening reading the journals.

When he arrived at the fire tower the sun was setting, bathing the mountaintops in a rosy light. At the tower's base was a small cabin. Inside there was a fireplace, a bunk, and a table. The single cupboard was only partially stocked. Matt dug out a can of beans and ate them cold. After supper, he filled the kerosene light, unrolled his sleeping bag, and stretched out on the bunk.

He glanced quickly through the first journal, but it was the second one he really wished to study. Its discovery had been very important to Katy, and he wondered what it had revealed to her. He turned his attention to it.

It was dated October, 1905, the year, as he later learned, of Takseen's death—one year after the marriage of her only child, John, whom Katy had known affectionately as Grandpa John.

Matt was touched, as Katy had been, at the loving dedication old Sam Ketchum had expressed for his Nez Perce wife Takseen, or Sarah. He read quickly through the undamaged opening pages, but then he too was slowed by the stained and blotted section that followed.

Only because he was knowledgeable about Nez Perce history could Matt piece together the story of the fateful journey undertaken by the Nez Perce—the tragic crossing of the Snake River, the Lolo ordeal, and the ironic courtship of Takseen and Buffalo Robe, whose marriage plans were tragically unfulfilled.

Matt's eyes were growing tired and he drew the kerosene lamp closer as he continued the account, written in Sam Ketchum's rambling style.

One day not long ago I found Takseen crying. I asked her to tell me why. It was then that she told me the secret she had kept within her Heart for more than a year. It seems that a year or two ago, we happened across some Injun cousins of hers while trapping, and she found out from them that the graves of nearly all the Nez Perce dead at the Big Hole battlefield were later dug up, that the bodies were mutilated. It wasn't General Howard or Colonel Gibbon's men; I'll say that for them. Now Takseen never had any proof that Buffalo Robe's grave was disturbed, and she never told me her suspicions at first, but she pestered me every now and again to go back to the Big Hole, Iskumtselalik Pah, she called it. But never till that day I found her crying did she bring herself to tell me why.

For an Injun, to have his grave disturbed is a terrible thing. His Soul wanders forever until those bones are restored. For that reason, Takseen had worried herself Sick about the remains of her Warrior. Course, we'd been married nigh unto twenty years before she learned what might have happened to Buffalo Robe's grave. Naturally, she was a mite Timid to ask me, her Husband, to help restore the grave of the Injun she almost Married.

Just the same, when I found out the true reason for her Desire to return to the Big Hole, I agreed to go. God only knows I meant what I told her, but now she lays sick and dying, and I never kept that promise to her. May God forgive me.

Anyhow, her Warrior Buffalo Robe had done a fine job of fighting in the siege that followed the dawn attack. He Distinguished himself in battle as Takseen was later told by Eyewitnesses.

This is how Buffalo Robe's story went. Remember, the day of the Big Hole Massacre was to have been the day of his marriage to Takseen. A corner of her Heart was always reserved for the memory of her Warrior, so when she learned the facts I'm about to set pen to, she reported them to me with gentle Tears of Remembrance and Trembling voice.

The white soldiers, after their brutal attack on the sleeping village, retreated to the hilltop above the river. They were equipped with trowel-like bayonets and used these to dig trenches into the hilltop. Buffalo Robe and the other Injun sharpshooters held good positions by that time and made short shrift of many of those soldiers in their shallow trenches. Takseen's Warrior was concealed in the branches of a pine and his marksmanship accounted for two dead early in the battle. There would have been more, but his good friend Rattle-on-Blanket's cries of distress forced him from his concealed position. With a mighty war cry he rushed in to give battle with his *kopluts* to the two long knives who had cornered Rattle-on-Blanket. The first soldier swung his rifle like a club and knocked Rattle-on-Blanket to the ground. Then they both turned to Buffalo Robe. Buffalo Robe did not understand the meaning of the words shouted by a White officer to the two attackers. "Back off!" the long knife shouted to them. One, who had been circling Buffalo Robe with a knife, suddenly backed off just as Buffalo Robe swung his *kopluts* and knocked the second attacker to the ground. At the same instant the Fatal bullet was launched from the officer's rifle, striking Buffalo Robe in the chest.

"I am hit!" he called to his friend Rattle-on-Blanket who was just then getting to his feet.

"Death to the Red Dogs!" the soldiers cried, moving in for the kill. The first had his bayonet ready, aimed for a fatal thrust to Rattle-on-Blanket's chest. The officer swung his rifle butt viciously at Buffalo Robe's head, but there was no further need for Brutality.

Buffalo Robe had no chance to sing his final Death Song. If he had it would have been lost in the din of Battle. The survivor who reported these things to Takseen told how the smells of smoke and Death and the cries of the Dying continued without Surcease while the Soul of Buffalo Robe quietly returned to its Earth Mother.

As the afternoon wore on, the cries of soldiers, sick with thirst and hunger, were added to the noise. It was given to Lone Coyote to find the body of Takseen's Warrior, and to those two Bereaved fell the dreadful task of burying the Dead. Lone Coyote rode into camp, the body of Buffalo Robe lying across the back of a pack horse. The Horrible sights that greeted his old eyes must have made his Heart sick, for there in the camp he discovered the bodies of all his beloved ones, Gray Deer, his infant daughter, and the wife of his youth, Broken Wing. His own shoulder wound went unheeded while he and

Takseen prepared shallow graves in a ravine, gently laying the bodies of their dear ones to rest. Their final task was to plant saplings above the graves in order to conceal them from possible disturbance.

Matt set the journal aside for a moment. His eyes were smarting. "The light is just too bad in here," he told himself, but the tear that ran from the corner of his eye forced him to acknowledge how moved he was by the journal's account of the Big Hole tragedy.

A coyote yipped on a nearby mountainside and was answered by a similar call from across the valley. Reassured by the familiar sound and brought back momentarily to the present, Matt again took up the journal and continued reading.

Concealing the graves was all for naught, as it turned out. Survivors later learned that the Bannock Indians searched out the hastily buried dead. Some Fifty or more bodies had been laid within the protection of willow trees overhanging the river bank. These and others were discovered when wolves and carrion-eating birds led the Desecrators to the remains of the dead. If Buffalo Robe was one of those found, as he surely must have been, he suffered horrible Mutilation, God rest his Soul. According to Injun belief, as I have aforementioned, his hapless Soul was released to eternal unhappy wanderings, once his bones were disturbed.

The sun was streaming through the single window of the cabin when Matt awoke. He didn't remember where the journal had left off and dreaming had begun, but his sleep had been troubled. He felt as though he had personally witnessed the scenes enacted a century ago.

A poor night's sleep did nothing to inhibit the plan he had formulated. There was no doubt in his mind about the task he and Katy had to accomplish as he set about preparing for the return journey.

He closed the journal that lay open on the bunk and placed it in the tin box with the other. Within a few minutes he stood briefly in the shadow of the fire tower, automatically surveying the surrounding timber for signs of smoke, then started down the rocky trail to headquarters.

13

"I'll agree to your plan," Jane Ketchum said to Matt in the hospital coffeeshop. "God only knows I'm desperate enough."

"Thank you, Mrs. Ketchum." Appreciation and relief showed in his face. Matt took a last sip of coffee. "Now, to convince Dr. Langley to discharge Katy . . ."

He excused himself to seek out Katy's doctor. While he looked up and down the corridors, Matt pondered the strange turn Katy had taken. She'd regained consciousness and her body had healed, but an emotional problem lingered, coupled with trance-like states in which she lost awareness of her surroundings. It was possible that the blow she'd received to her head was responsible for her unpredictable behavior. At least, that was how the doctor explained it. Matt had a solution of his own which he was about to propose to Dr. Langley.

He saw the white-jacketed doctor walking down the hall, charts in hand, joking with the nurse who was assisting him on rounds.

"Excuse me, Dr. Langley. May I talk to you for a minute?"

"Is it Katy again, Matt?" The alarm in his voice was a measure of his concern for his patient.

"Nothing in her conddition has changed, but I'd like to discuss a possible solution." He studied the pleasant face of the doctor, who had worked patiently and well with Katy over the past two weeks. "I know you're puzzled by the strange way Katy has been behaving for the last two days. I think I may have the answer."

Dr. Langley raised his eyebrows.

"Katy must be discharged and allowed to go with me as a condition of her recovery."

The shocked look on Dr. Langley's face caused Matt once again to regret his bluntness.

"I'll tell you, Matt. Quite frankly, she's physically capable of leaving, but in her present disoriented state—well, I could hardly consent to discharge her."

"You'll excuse me for saying this, doctor, but there are no psychiatric facilities in this hospital. What further treatment can you provide for her here?"

"Are you proposing to take her to another hospital? If so, why, of course I'd be happy to make a referral." Dr. Langley dismissed the nurse before Matt answered.

"Not another hospital," Matt said. "I'm thinking of taking her to the place that might have the effect of psychologically jolting her back to the present."

"I'm not sure I follow you."

"I can't explain it fully. If you would just consent to discharge her, I think I could help. You see, the things she has been saying, incoherent though they may sound, have meaning to me. She is apparently very distressed over a situation that occurred in the past. I know I can ease her mind by taking her to the place where this distressing event happened. When she realizes she no longer has cause to worry, her peace of mind may be restored. Incidentally, I have her mother's consent for this plan."

The doctor paused a moment. "What you have told me is a little vague, about as vague as the young lady has been. However, I can't forcibly restrain either her or you. I'm willing to make an arrangement. Since I can foresee no physical reasons for keeping her longer, I'll release her. Because I have grown to respect you a great deal over these past two weeks, I'll entrust her to your care. There are certain symptoms, however, that it will be necessary for you to watch for. You must promise to bring her back if any of these occur, and you must have her back for a checkup in ten days regardless."

Matt nodded while the doctor set forth his conditions. Finally they shook hands and Matt was free to give Katy the good news.

When he entered her room, he saw Katy seated beside the window, wearing a pretty yellow bed jacket. Her long black hair fell softly about her shoulders, and her skin, though pallid beneath the fading tan, looked healthy.

"Matt?" She gave him a pretty, puzzled smile. "You tell me to call you Matt, yet I can't dispel the feeling that you're someone else." She shook her head and passed a hand across her eyes. "I feel so strange, so unsure of myself. Sometimes I'm not even sure who I am."

She lapsed into silence.

The doctor had tried to explain her spells of uncertainty by the blow to the head. He theorized that it was even possible that the material in the journal had had such a powerful emotional impact on her that her mind had locked in on it at the moment of the accident. Such a situation could make her literally a prisoner of the past.

That was the doctor's theory, but Matt thought otherwise privately. His reasons would be scoffed at if he tried to explain them, especially with his inability to express things convincingly. Instead, he simply kept his plan in his heart, along with the knowledge of Katy's vision-like dream at Moose Meadow. Katy had dreamed of her mission to restore the bones of Buffalo Robe, and back at the fire tower Matt had experienced the same emotional involvement with Takseen's story. He too felt charged with the task of restoring Buffalo Robe's soul to its earth mother. Moreover, he felt he could be the instrument through whom the ill-fated relationship of a century earlier could be resolved. That was a dream he could only cherish in his heart for the time being. If he and Katy had indeed known one another in a previous life, separated by a cruel fate, then perhaps there was such a thing as a second chance.

Those were private thoughts, and even Jane Ketchum didn't know his innermost reasons for the journey he wished to undertake with Katy. Jane was willing to accept the doctor's supposition that her daughter was still in a confused state, still living the contents of the journal that had been so heavily on her mind when the accident occurred.

"Katy, we're going back now. Are you ready?"

She nodded, a smile on her face for the first time. Yet her large blue eyes still had a haunted, pleading look about them. She sat on the edge of the bed, a suitcase on the floor beside her. The bed was elevated, and Katy, with her feet swinging above the floor, wearing levis and an embroidered peasant blouse, looked a little like a small, lost child.

Matt's heart went out to her. Her mental state had deteriorated and she had regressed more and more into the past, at times making statements that astounded him because they contained knowledge it seemed impossible she could know, even had she completed reading the second journal.

For the most part, however, she was silent, sadly, patiently waiting for the journey Matt had promised her a day earlier.

Dr. Langley stepped in to say good-by. Matt detected a

touch of anxiety in the doctor's face as he fondly bade farewell to the girl whose life he had saved, but whose mind, locked in on the past, he had been unable to reach.

Matt had secured permission to drive the forest service pickup. They loaded their gear and were soon bouncing across a back road that would take them crosscountry, directly to the Lolo Trail.

A short time later they were journeying down the trail, which had been converted into the twentieth-century Lewis and Clark Highway. Matt watched Katy closely for any signs of recognition of the scenic valley through which they were passing.

She was in the detached state that by then had grown very familiar. Matt found it best to talk to her as if she were the Indian girl of the journal.

"Katy," he addressed her, "do you recall the terrible journey across this trail? Is anything familiar to you?"

"It was raining then. I can't tell. We were high above the valley, up on the ridge. It has changed so much that nothing looks the same except the mountains themselves. This isn't the same trail."

Though Katy was living in the past, she was seemingly unperplexed by the inconsistencies—the great jump in time between the period she was reliving and the modern surroundings—the truck, the highway, the speed of their travel. Her mind shut out what she couldn't grasp and dwelled only on the single purpose she hoped to accomplish.

The Lolo Pass into Montana was a far cry from the treacherous goat path Takseen's people had followed in order to bypass the handful of defenders behind their improvised log barricade. The place was marked a hundred years later by a sign that described the events. The site of the fiasco had since become known as Fort Fizzle.

Matt stopped the truck to give Katy a chance to look around, but he said nothing. Before she had even read the historical marker Katy's eyes lit up in recognition.

"There were logs here!" she cried. "The soldiers tried to stop us. The soldiers and those traitor Indians who fought for them." She pointed to the side of the mountain above them. "Up there is where we camped, and in that meadow over there Joseph and the other chiefs held council with the white leaders." She shook her head sadly. "It was no use. They wanted us to surrender. So we marched past them on a narrow trail high above." She looked dreamily into the distance as her mind relived the event. "I remember now. We were singing as we passed above them. It was a great joke on the white soldiers!"

Matt was truly startled at her "memory." Judging from Katy's notebook, in which she had begun to copy from the second journal, she had read no more than the opening pages. She had no first-hand knowledge of Sam Ketchum's account of the trek.

They were soon out of the pass and into Montana, heading south through the Bitterroot Valley.

The broad valley lay between high mountains. It was populated by small towns. Some of them had been there when the Nez Perce had passed through the valley a hundred years earlier, but those settlements too had changed, and if Katy recognized anything, she kept it in her heart.

Finally she nodded as if satisfied that they were indeed in the right place. "Ket-la-met-a-lee," she said. "This is the same Bitterroot Valley. It too has changed, but the white people will never destroy its beauty. We were happy here. We felt safe."

She said little else, but as they drew closer to the Big Hole battlefield she became agitated.

Within the hour, Matt pulled into the parking lot of the

visitor center. The battle site had become recognized as a national battlefield, and an impressive structure stood atop the hill.

"Here we are, Katy. Are you ready?"

"Yes."

Matt asked her to remain in the truck while he made inquiries with the personnel at the information desk. He had taken the precaution of wearing his uniform, hoping the officials would be more amenable to his request.

When he first entered the building Matt gave a start of recognition. Through the panoramic expanse of windows lay the scene of the battlefield, precisely as the journal had detailed it. His own knowledge of the event, even his dreams, were so closely interwoven with the journal account and with Katy's living dream that it was difficult for him to separate them. For a moment he felt such a close sense of identification with the scene that it was hard to remember he was only a visitor.

At his request a park service employee led him into a small office adjacent to the information desk. Matt explained that he had a girl with him whose great-grandmother had been on the trek with Joseph and that her ancestor had lost many loved ones in the massacre. Without saying anything that would be an embarrassment to Katy, Matt explained that she had knowledge of some burial spots through old family journals, and that her family's graves had been among those desecrated after their burial. Matt told him further that Katy had been disturbed by that knowledge for a long time, and had long desired to journey to the site to see if anything remained of the graves.

"Sort of a pilgrimage, as I understand it." The park official nodded sympathetically. "We don't normally allow visitors to roam the grounds outside the marked trails. However, under the circumstances," he tapped his fingers together,

"I would be pleased to make an exception. Of course someone will accompany you."

Matt knew the arrangements had been going too smoothly and he was prepared for such a suggestion. He shifted in his chair. "Well, sir, if I may just say this. You see, for the young lady, this pilgrimage is intensely personal, and to have a stranger present would be very upsetting to her."

The other man nodded thoughtfully.

"If you're concerned about our disturbing anything," Matt continued, "you may rest assured that we'll do no damage. In fact, we may be able to add to your knowledge of what went on here a hundred years ago."

That last reasoning appealed to the official. "I'm willing to forego the assistant in your case. Of course, any finds you make, artifacts and the like, must remain on the property and their whereabouts reported. Agreed?"

"Agreed," Matt said, extending his hand and breathing an inward sigh of relief.

Katy was sitting in the truck, still in an agitated state, wringing her hands. Matt helped her out the door and picked up a small satchel. There was a small folding shovel among its contents that he didn't particularly want the information employee to see.

They followed a marked trail down a hill to where it crossed the Big Hole River and led to the siege site. Off to the right, on the near side of the river, swept the broad expanse of open meadow, butting up against the river and the willow clumps where the main slaughter took place.

Suddenly Matt detected a trembling in Katy. She pointed to the timbered hill across the bridge. "I won't go up there, Matt." She stood frozen in place and the trembling became a violent shaking.

"You don't have to, little one," he told her, putting a gentle arm around her shoulders.

"Evil spirits. There are evil spirits there. Much bad fighting. Many dead."

He led her away from the place that had frightened her, and they made their way across the grassy prairie to the village site.

The skies had been darkening gradually in the past hour and a steady wind was blowing, bending the grass in undulating movements. Ominous clouds appeared on the horizon, and the handful of visitors on the trail left the siege site in a flurry to reach their cars before the storm broke.

"Do you want to wait in the truck until this blows over?"

Katy emphatically shook her head no. She bit her lips and walked stiffly toward the scene of the disaster, her eyes straight ahead. Then she stopped and took in the panorama, pointing to the edge of the river. "Here is where our wedding lodge stood. And there," pointing again, "that was the hospital lodge where Broken Wing was shot. All over, smoke, and shooting, and screaming people. Soldiers coming from the willows across the river. But then our braves found their rifles. They forced the soldiers up the hill, across the river. They captured the enemy's great gun, the thunder bird, but it was no good. Many brave warriors died. My father was wounded. Buffalo Robe, my betrothed . . ." Her voice trailed off as if the painful recollection was too much to bear.

Her eyes searched the hillside with its numerous ravines. Then she turned resolutely, her arm outstretched toward a narrow ravine, and pointed. The wind was coming strongly now, pressing her thin blouse against her, but she no longer shivered. In a controlled voice that summed up a generation of tragedy she said, "We shall dig there."

Matt nodded and they made their way down an incline and, taking off their shoes, splashed across the shallow river.

By then the sky was completely black. The lights of the visitor center had gone out in an electrical failure, and even the headlights of the visitors' cars had disappeared. The wind suddenly stopped, and an oppressive silence hung in the air as they made their way up the ravine.

There was no hesitation in Katy's steps. She scrambled up over rocks and around the scrub oak until she came to the place where a full-grown pine stood entirely alone. There was no mounding of the earth to indicate that that was the place, but Katy nodded quietly, almost imperceptibly, and Matt got out the shovel.

The air was charged with tension as the storm held off yet a little longer. The wind held itself suspended, ready to begin its keening at any moment; but in the deathly stillness a new keening replaced the sound of the wind; a haunting wailing came from Katy's lips, softly at first, then rising to a weeping crescendo, the death song of a squaw. It rose and carried across the valley, haunting, wild, and unearthly. Yet there was dignity in the cry, as a hundred years of pent-up emotion spilled forth across the waiting battlefield.

14

"We've come many miles, sister. I doubt more than ever the wisdom of this route," confided Yellow Moccasin wearily from the back of Spotted Eagle.

Even though twelve suns had passed since the Big Hole, it was an effort for Takseen to answer. Sadness rose and choked her like a living thing whenever she broke her silence.

"We couldn't travel in the direction of the rising sun, little brother. Too many forts."

The route of the straggling survivors of the Big Hole had taken them south and east toward the Yellowstone. They were approaching the southwest side of Henry's Lake to spend a day resting before crossing Targhee Pass and dropping into the Yellowstone.

Henry's Lake was a fine lake, a place where food was bountiful, but the peacefulness of the setting did not lull the Nez Perce into a false sense of security such as they had experienced at the Big Hole.

"Little brother, it won't be long now until we're in the land of our brothers, the Mountain Crows. Then we shall test the wisdom of journeying so far south."

"I've heard Ollokut say that if we're not satisfied living amongst the Crows, we'll have an easy plains crossing straight north into Canada."

"Yes, perhaps an easy crossing, but many, many miles to cover for our weary people."

Later Yellow Moccasin helped his sister gather wood for the cooking fire. They would spend the night close beside it, wrapped in blankets. Although three moons ago Yellow Moccasin would have been insulted to help with a woman's work, all things had changed since the massacre. Everyone did what work he could to fill the gaps left by the loss of loved ones. Indeed, one warrior had tallied more than eighty casualties on his buffalo-horn drinking cup, and scarcely a family was untouched by personal loss.

Yellow Moccasin, whose leg had partially healed, gathered his fishing gear, a net and some hemp cord, and he told his sister he would be back later.

For a moment Takseen held Yellow Moccasin with her sad dark eyes, sorrowing for the responsibilities that had been thrust upon him before he was fully a man.

"This is when I miss Father," she said in a choked voice. She found it nearly impossible to speak of those terrible days.

The slanting rays of the setting sun bathed the boy in their light, and as he mutely nodded, the tears that fell upon his cheek were turned to gold. He turned, visibly straightening his shoulders, and limped toward the lake and the small stream that flowed into it.

Takseen too decided to spend the remaining daylight time gathering food, and with her pack basket she set out alone to gather roots and bulbs, even aspen bark. There had been insufficient time for good gathering on the hasty retreat from the Big Hole, and her stomach was crying for nourishment.

In her solitary task Takseen could not ward off the memories that flooded over her. She and Yellow Moccasin had buried Lone Coyote five suns from the Big Hole. He had died simply for lack of time to rest properly and to receive the care he needed. His was only one of many bodies buried beside the trail, dead from wounds incurred at the Big Hole. Their suffering had been intense as those wounded ones made the difficult journey, dragged on travois behind horses. Though Lone Coyote's shoulder wound had bled profusely, infection set in and he died a painful death. Perhaps with the skill of Broken Wing, had she been alive, his death could have been avoided, but Takseen had given up wondering what might have been.

She could barely take pleasure in the news two days earlier of the daring night attack Ollokut and twenty-eight others had made upon Howard's men at Kamisnim Takin, Camas Meadows. There the warriors had run off an entire pack string, forcing General Howard into yet another delay while he had to scour the countryside to purchase replacements. Takseen managed a small inward smile in her knowledge that both Lone Coyote and Buffalo Robe would have delighted in participating in that raid. The well-planned maneuver had indeed taken the long knives by surprise.

That night Takseen and Yellow Moccasin dined on fresh fish, and Pale Moon's family, who had lost none of its male providers, contributed a sage grouse to the cooking pot. With a full stomach and meat assured for yet another day, Takseen and Yellow Moccasin wrapped themselves in blankets, and with their feet to the fire, fell asleep beneath a canopy of stars.

It wasn't until the Yellowstone that a small incident occurred that caused Takseen to withdraw from her state of mourning enough to take note of the plight of another woman. That other woman was white; her name was Emma Cowan.

Since entering the Yellowstone, the Indians had been on the lookout for whites who could guide them through the unfamiliar park. The United States government had set the land aside five years earlier as a national park, and there were occasional groups of campers to be found within its boundaries.

Emma Cowan was a member of such a party. Takseen learned later that Emma and her husband George and her thirteen-year-old sister Ida had joined a group of friends to see for themselves the unnatural wonders of Yellowstone Park that summer of 1877.

Takseen watched curiously as the white women were led into camp. It was late in the day and the Indians were encamped on the fringes of a circular basin. A thousand or more ponies were pastured within the shelter of the basin whose rim was circled by campfires. Emma and Ida watched just as curiously at the bustle of camp activity, for still more ponies were being driven in for unpacking.

After dark Takseen stood quietly by her fire, warming her hands against the September chill, silently watching the white woman. She had learned from a member of the group who had captured them that the Cowan party of eight had been surprised that morning at breakfast. To appease the Indians, the tourists had supplied the warriors with a hearty breakfast of flapjacks and had given them a supply of bacon and flour. The warriors still weren't appeased, and they eyed the well-rested horses belonging to the whites. The party was captured and taken to Chief Looking Glass, who released them minus their horses. Their harrowing day was not over; they were next recaptured by another group of young men. Two of their party escaped and some were wounded. Ultimately only Emma and Ida and their brother Frank were retained, that time being taken to Joseph. Emma by that time was wild with fear, having left her husband, George, for dead when the warriors had shattered his leg with a bullet, then shot him in the forehead to put him out of his misery.

Knowing the agony the white woman was suffering caused a mixture of feelings within Takseen's breast. She felt general hatred for all white people for the sufferings they had inflicted on her people; yet here was a woman who had suffered as she had—losing a loved one. Her sympathy overrode her hatred when she saw the fear in the woman's face.

The female captives were unsupervised, so Takseen motioned the women to her fire and indicated that they should warm themselves. The women approached but kept a nervous eye on their brother Frank, who was being brought before Joseph. By the expression of the chief's face, Takseen knew that he too disapproved of bringing any harm to the tourists. With a motion of disgust at hearing what had happened to the other whites, Joseph abruptly left the white man.

Springtime had by that time joined her friend and the white women, and Emma held out her arms for Springtime's infant daughter. The mother smiled at Emma, and in that flash of understanding between the two, Takseen saw that perhaps her people and the whites were not completely dissimilar. That brief moment of understanding created the first softening of the shell into which Takseen had withdrawn after the tragic massacre.

She realized that her heart was further changing on the following morning when the hostages were released. She watched as Lean Elk ordered the hostages to mount the worn-out horses that had been provided for them.

Takseen stepped up to Emma Cowan as the women mounted the horses. "Take this," she said, extending a small covered basket to the nervous white woman. "Food for you," she explained, and the woman smiled in appreciation for the berries and leaf-wrapped pieces of meat.

Emma was still clearly apprehensive as she drew her shawl

about her shoulders. Takseen thought the party had more to fear from the wild young warriors than from Joseph's peaceable people.

Lean Elk led them off toward the river, where the trail entered the deep timber. Takseen watched the group out of sight, apprehensive for their safety. She never learned what became of them.

While small bands of young men continued to harass any tourists they discovered, the main body of the Nez Perce moved across the Yellowstone River and along the north shore of the lake, then followed a tributary by the name of Pelican Creek toward the Stinking Water.

It was near the Stinking Water that Joseph got word of the presence of soldiers under the command of Colonel Samuel D. Sturgis. With the benefit of this intelligence, Joseph executed another brilliant outflanking maneuver, and amidst the wild timbered ridges, towering gorges, and abrupt chasms of that wilderness country, he managed to avoid the Colonel completely, passing between Sturgis' men and the forces of General Howard, who were also closing in.

The knowledge that the whites were close behind was only half the bad news. By that time, the Nez Perce had become aware that the Mountain Crows, their old allies, were remaining neutral throughout the conflict, and the River Crows had declared themselves on the side of the army.

When Looking Glass brought this news to camp there was much agitation.

Joseph, in agreement with the other chiefs, concluded that night, "We have no choice but to go to the Old Woman's country." The people nodded, but they were discouraged. The Canadian border to which he referred was many suns' journey from the Yellowstone country.

A series of rainy days set in, ushering in the unpredictable

September weather. The trails became slippery. The rugged terrain was both an ally and an enemy, for while it delayed the Nez Perce retreat, it slowed the soldiers even more.

It was the middle of the month when the Nez Perce again halted for a rest camp. They had chosen a narrow wash with vertical banks ten to twenty feet high. That place, known as Canyon Creek, was dry despite the unseasonal rains.

The Nez Perce no longer allowed themselves to feel a false sense of security. Lookouts guarded all possible access points to the encampment. Nevertheless, there was little advance notice of Sturgis's attack. The only warning the weary people had was a scout's blanket signal. The scout warned the warriors as he rode in short circles, waving his blanket. Only minutes later more than three hundred soldiers were suddenly upon them, mounted, charging toward the Indian encampment.

For Takseen, the next step was by then routine. She joined the other women, children, and old ones in packing up camp and scurrying up the canyon while the warriors, secluded behind rocks and brush, defended the entrance to it.

Yellow Moccasin remained behind to drive the pony herd within the shelter of the canyon. It was clear that the canyon was a good place from which to defend themselves, for it grew even narrower upstream and was overhung by ledges.

Takseen, alone when her brother remained behind, hastened to tighten the cinch on her saddle.

"Come with us. Are you ready?" It was the urgent voice of Pale Moon summoning Takseen.

She mounted and nudged her mare's flanks. "I'm ready." Driving her pack ponies ahead of her, Takseen joined Pale Moon and her mother and younger sisters.

They made their way up the canyon, but a few soldiers, firing from the rim of the bluff, tried to turn them back.

There were cries as the bullets struck home. Takseen did not know the two women who were killed or the others who were crippled by the fire.

The band of noncombatants kept up their weary pace through the entire day and all of the next night. It wasn't until Yellow Moccasin returned to the main band that Takseen learned the bad news concerning the horse herd.

"We failed, sister," he told Takseen sadly. His shoulders slumped, and from his face Takseen judged he was assuming the entire burden for the mishap.

"Just after we got the main herd into the canyon, the soldiers pushed close upon us. We were forced to abandon nearly four hundred ponies." Yellow Moccasin sighed. "They were the tired ones. We had to do it in order to save the others."

Takseen laid a gentle hand on Yellow Moccasin's shoulder. She longed to pull him close and comfort him as she would a son, but Yellow Moccasin was too proud. During that summer he had become a man. His figure had broadened, and though he still had seen only thirteen snows, the responsibilities he had borne through the terrible events of the past months had changed him.

Takseen could only offer him a cold meal, and that was little comfort.

After a short rest the families moved early. It was along the Elk River that the first strange Indians appeared. They were not the Nez Perce's friends, the Walk-Around Sioux or the Snakes, as the scouts first thought. They were River Crows. Here was a new enemy, one which had formerly been an ally.

There were close to a hundred Indians who carried on a running battle with the Nez Perce warriors, sniping at them from horseback. They fired at each other, hanging low alongside their horses, shooting under the necks of the animals.

They galloped hard, and the battle continued over many miles.

Again the families endeavored to stay ahead, protected by scouts and warriors in the rear who kept back the persistent Crows.

They were a day's journey from the Musselshell River when the Crows finally ceased pursuit. The Nez Perce had abandoned another five hundred ponies who were too weary to continue. The Crows ran them off and, satisfied with that prize, quit the conflict.

Yet there was still no rest for the people. Takseen had pushed her pack ponies hard for a hundred and fifty miles. The Crows were no longer a menace, but Colonel Sturgis and his men had not given up pursuit. They had merely traveled at a slower pace, letting the Crows do the harassing.

It was several days before the Indians judged they had left Sturgis safely behind. Having safely outdistanced the white soldiers, the Nez Perce clung once again to the feeble promise of freedom to the north.

15

The pace was unbroken in the next days. The incident that stood out most vividly in Takseen's memory was the skirmish at Cow Island. For eighteen hours, the young men had laid siege to a small garrison. While they had been unable to dislodge its occupants, the Indians were at least able to replenish their waning supplies from the freight depot.

Fortunately for the Nez Perce, the garrison had just received a large supply of government and private freight. After stocking their own larders, the warriors set fire to the rest and proceeded on their way.

Shortly afterwards, they were pursued by a small detachment of cavalry. About ten miles north of the Cow Island garrison, the mounted soldiers engaged the Indians.

Once again the warriors held them off. In a skirmish lasting only two hours they made each shot count while the main band made good its escape.

In camp that night Yellow Moccasin complained to his sister. "I wish I had fought with our braves. I wouldn't have let them go so easily. We could have picked off every one of them."

Takseen tried to explain, though in her heart she wasn't sure she shared the still peaceable intentions of Joseph. "Joseph does not start the fights. He wants only for us to get to the buffalo country. We fight just to protect ourselves until we can safely cross into the Old Woman's country."

"It isn't many sun's journey ahead, is it, my sister?"

"Only a few more suns."

The country through which they had been passing since crossing the Musselshell was grass-covered prairie, dry and rolling, cut at intervals by crooked ravines. They had left the rains behind and there was little water in the sage- and cactus-strewn plains, but where the river flowed, the banks were lined with cottonwoods. In spite of the dryness there was bunch grass in abundance for grazing. Buffalo were also plentiful, so that the people, as well as the ponies, had full stomachs.

After the skirmishes at Cow Island, with the soldiers always at least two marches behind, the Indians felt more certain of their goal, but there were some among them who disagreed about the slowness of the pace.

Lean Elk, who had assumed much of the leadership since the Big Hole slaughter, was in favor of pressing steadily on to the border, but Looking Glass, who had been relieved of some of his authority after the massacre, wished to slow up.

It was a cold stormy night when Takseen listened to the arguments around the campfires.

"I tell you," Looking Glass, said, "General Howard is several days behind. We have food now from the white men's supply station. The buffalo are plentiful, and our people are near exhaustion. Look," he gestured toward the black sky. "Do you not feel the breath of winter coming on?"

"How will it help us to be caught up by the blizzards?" Lean Elk angrily questioned the handsome young chieftain.

"We will not be caught. Better to have full stomachs and strong bodies to ward off the cold. There is no hurry."

Lean Elk shrugged his shoulders in resignation. "And I tell you," he said to Looking Glass, "you can lead again. I am trying to save the people, doing my best to cross into Canada before the soldiers find us. You can take command, but I think we will be caught and killed."

Takseen felt a tightening of fear in her chest. That the council agreed to the changes, to shorter marches, seemed a foolish plan to her. How could they so quickly forget the bitter lesson of the Big Hole?

For four days the people made only a few miles at a time. They crossed the pass between the Little Rockies and the Bear Paws, and on the last day of September, with the chill north wind blowing from Canada, they halted on the northern slopes of the Bear Paw Mountains.

"This is a beautiful land," Pale Moon told her friend as the two girls began unpacking the ponies.

"Yes, and cold, but we're only an easy day's march from the Old Woman's country," Takseen answered.

"One more day to freedom."

The girls looked at each other, but Takseen felt the uneasy tightening again in her chest and she dared not smile. Looking Glass had insisted on a night camp though it was only noon. The forward scouts had brought down some buffalo on the banks of Snake Creek, and the people were anticipating full stomachs that night. Scattered opposition to Looking Glass' proposal wasn't vocal enough to prevent camp from being established in that place.

Takseen, who had grown skillful in recognizing campsites from the standpoint of defense, realized that Snake Creek was not easily defendable. A southern ridge provided the only protection; all other sides lay open to attack. Ravines and gullies slashed the rolling ground in a mazelike pattern, and though those scars in the landscape could act as protective entrenchments, they were inadequate to prevent a sense of vulnerability.

The girls established their respective camps and moved into the hills in search of firewood. It was scarce, but they found an adequate substitute in the abundant buffalo chips. Having gathered a great quantity of fuel, Takseen and Pale Moon set to work roasting some choice buffalo steaks. Takseen tried to set aside her fears and enjoy another welcome chance to recuperate.

It was early the next morning that Yellow Moccasin stirred within his blanket. The north wind had not abated and the chill night made him long for his warm tepee.

"Sister, it's too cold to sleep longer. Stir the fire while I check on Spotted Eagle. A piece of warm meat would taste good when I return."

So saying, the boy wrapped himself in a double blanket and, still limping noticeably, covered the frost-covered ground between the village and the pony herd. Though the sun had risen, its warmth had not yet thawed the white crystals that clung to every blade of grass.

Takseen rose to prepare her brother's breakfast. Yellow Moccasin was the only man in the family, and she was satisfied to take orders from him.

She knelt on the frozen earth and blew hard on the remains of the fire, her breath fogging in the chilly air. The embers glowed red, then burst into flames that caught the fresh fuel that she placed atop them. She was still concentrating on the fire when she heard Yellow Moccasin's cry of alarm.

"Cheyenne scouts! Soldiers! Pick up your rifles. We are attacked!" He galloped through camp on Spotted Eagle, waving his blanket in the frenzied motion that signaled attack.

These were not soldiers they had engaged before, as Takseen later discovered. Her people were being intercepted by Colonel Miles's cavalry, who had marched crosscountry from Fort Keogh in eastern Montana. Their arrival came as a complete surprise to the unsuspecting Indians, who had thought only to keep ahead of General "Day-After-Tomorrow" for one more day.

She looked up in time to see mounted soldiers, hundreds of them, galloping across the rolling prairie in a concerted charge against the encampment. They were nearly upon the village and would have struck with no warning had Yellow Moccasin's sharp eyes not spotted the Cheyenne scouts who were riding ahead of the cavalry.

Cutting a wide swathe across the undulating prairie, they charged in a vast precision movement with the sound of a stampeding buffalo herd.

"This is the day we will die," Takseen thought with finality as the mounted soldiers thundered closer. She automatically fingered the amulet at her breast, wondering how her life could possibly be preserved again. Pale Moon was at her side for a brief instant when both of them had the same thought.

"The horses!"

There were few enough men and able-bodied boys left, and the girls could do a man's work. Casting aside her blanket, Takseen untethered her mare and galloped alongside Pale Moon to the rim of the plateau behind the village where the ponies grazed. The animals were by that time used to the sound of gunfire, and they betrayed little nervousness as the warriors hastily entrenched themselves in the gullies that skirted the camp and began firing a deadly volley at close range.

While the Nez Perce sharpshooters continued to return the fire of the long knives, Takseen nudged her mare amidst the milling ponies and shouted at them to get moving.

Their numbers had been badly decimated as a result of the running battle with the River Crows and the Cow Island skirmish. It was important to move the remaining ponies within the boundaries of the encampment, for without them, there would be no possibility of flight to Canada.

The noise of the cavalry charge and the sound of the firing had risen to a high level. From the plateau Takseen could look down upon the warriors in their rifle pits. They continued to pick off the officers and men of Miles's cavalry. Other warriors were ranged along the low bluffs along one side of the encampment. There were clearly many casualties in the field, but not just on one side. The white marksmen were also taking their toll.

"Get moving," Takseen shouted above the sounds of battle. "Get along!" she cried to the ponies, which began to respond to the commands. There were others, including Yellow Moccasin, who were desperately trying to get the herd moving toward the village.

Takseen wheeled her horse and called out to Pale Moon to start moving. Simultaneously she became aware of an entire battalion that had swung to the rear of the village with the sole purpose of cutting off the horse herd.

Heedless of the fact that women were helping round up the horses, those soldiers began firing, drawing closer and mixing with the herd.

Takseen bent low over her horse's neck. "Let's go!" she cried to Pale Moon, but the girl didn't answer. She raised her head and looked to the rear.

"Aiee! I am struck!" Pale Moon clutched her head in blind agony. A bright stain seeped through her fingers and she slid limply from her horse.

She lay crumpled on the frozen ground, conscious a moment longer as Takseen dismounted and bent close above her. "Save yourself," the girl whispered to her friend. "Don't let the long knives catch you." She closed her eyes while her heart's blood spilled across the frozen earth. Then she was still.

Takseen shouted to Yellow Moccasin. He galloped to her side and dismounted, exclaiming, "Did you see this happen, sister?"

"No, I only heard her cry out. There was a soldier . . ."

"I saw it. It was not a soldier but a cowardly Cheyenne scout." He spat in disgust. "The man grabbed her bridle and shot her, then rode off."

While he spoke, Yellow Moccasin placed the body of Pale Moon across the back of her horse. "Get her back to camp. I'll move the pony herd."

Groups of warriors had seen the attempt to capture the horse herd, and they engaged the troops in a running battle. The braves managed to separate the battalion from the rest of the troops, but the white soldiers by then had driven off the horse herd. Takseen watched numbly for a moment while the sniping continued, sickened as the herd headed away from the village. She saw an officer's horse shot from beneath him. A trumpeter ran to his officer and held off the advancing warriors until the stunned captain recovered sufficiently to grab another mount.

The action moved off behind the camp and Takseen realized that the loss of the herd was final. With heavy heart she led Pale Moon's mare back to camp to return the body to the girl's loved ones.

The fighting was still close on all sides of the camp and the noise was terrible. The smell of smoke and powder was strong in her nostrils. For a terrible instant, as she made her way through the midst of the battle, Takseen believed herself to be back at the Big Hole, and a dreadful fear swept over her. She shook it aside. "I have nothing to lose," she thought. "I must make my heart brave."

From the wailing and sobbing that greeted her she realized the toll was heavy in camp, but she was stunned to learn that old Toohoohoolzote, along with Lean Elk, and Joseph's handsome brother Ollokut, were fatally struck down that day. Pile of Clouds, Hahtalekin, and others were also named among the dead, all leaders, all critically necessary for victory.

Singly and in pairs, in small squads, the defenders picked off officers and decimated the ranks of soldiers, but the enemy's numbers were too great. There were always more white men to take the place of those whose saddles emptied.

By the middle of the afternoon, the soldiers had suffered enough and withdrew under the withering fire. For the first time, Takseen had time to comfort the family of Pale Moon. She joined the weeping parents and younger sisters, but as she wept, it was more than the loss of her friend for whom the tears fell; it was for her mother, her father, her baby sister, Broken Wing, and all the others. Above all, she sorrowed for the loss of her beloved Buffalo Robe. The hurt was dredged up anew, like an open wound, as the sounds of mourning brought back that other, terrible day.

While the wailing for the dead echoed through the sorrowing camp, the temperature steadily dropped. A weak winter sun hovered on the horizon when Colonel Miles ringed the encampment with men in fixed positions, laying siege to the Indians.

Though the siege could take a possible future toll, it was unsuccessful in depriving the Indians of a water supply. Nor was it in time to prevent the daring escape of a hundred women and children and their warrior escort, members of White Bird's band, who had dashed past the attackers earlier in the day and made good their escape. The escorts, singly and in groups, had made their way back through the fighting lines once the women and children and their pack-laden ponies were on their way.

Takseen wondered, with night drawing on, how the fugitives were faring. The first flakes of snow were being whipped across the prairie by a bitter wind, and the sharp breath of winter was bearing down from the north. Occasional firing continued into the night, but for the most part, the combatants retired from active shooting with the coming of night.

Takseen had helped with Pale Moon's burial, and she reluctantly left the sorrowing family in order to help increase the fortifications. With camas hooks, knives, trowel bayonets taken from the soldiers at the Big Hole, even pans from the Cow Island supply depot, the women helped the warriors excavate jug-shaped foxholes for the fighting men and shelter pits for the women and children.

Under cover of darkness they worked well past the evening meal. It was fortunate that a system of coulees already existed. They managed, digging with numbed fingers and inadequate tools, to connect some of the rifle pits with underground tunnels.

Takseen worked alongside Yellow Moccasin. Her strenuous efforts prevented the cold from penetrating her body, but her heart went out to the little ones who were crying from cold and hunger.

It was long past nightfall when they stopped for a bite of supper. There could be no light, no cooking fires, to draw attention to their location, so supper consisted merely of bits of dried meat. Mothers passed the morsels first to their distressed children, and the little that remained they shared among themselves. The old people sat huddled in their blankets, saying nothing, but in their eyes a deep, silent misery showed.

Takseen refused a bit of dried meat that Springtime

offered her. "Save it for the little ones," she said. "When this battle is over, they must be numbered among the living." Takseen's voice was bitter. She held little hope for their survival. The chiefs, many of them, were killed that day. The horse herd was run off. Eighteen men and three women had lost their lives, and the presence of death was everywhere. The sounds of the death wail rose from the darkness while the wind drove mercilessly across the bleak plain.

Springtime leaned back against the wall of the shelter pit. Takseen watched while she nursed her infant—Joseph's daughter, less than four months old. The little one beat with tiny fists against her mother's breast and turned her head from side to side in anger because the milk would not come.

"I have so little milk for her," Springtime told Takseen. "Poor baby," and she stroked the warm brown head that nuzzled against her. It was many minutes before the baby was satisfied enough to drop into a restless slumber. Springtime rewrapped the child in her blankets, and held her close, crooning softly from their bed of freshly dug earth.

The baby slept, but other, older children were not so fortunate. They cried out in hunger, and wept from the cold until Takseen could no longer bear the sounds of their suffering.

Springtime slept at last, leaning against the back of the dirt wall, and Takseen left without disturbing her. She sought out Yellow Moccasin, and while he loosened dirt from the pits, she scooped it into a pan and carried it away to conceal the evidence of the fortifications.

None of the people could sleep long. The cold grew even more intense toward dawn, and with it came a full-fledged snowstorm. By daylight, snow lay on the ground and the fuel, consisting of scant brush and buffalo chips, lay buried beneath snow the depth of ten fingers, belying the fact that the camp was known as Tsanim Alikos Pah, Place of the Manure Fire.

In the first light of dawn, the bodies of the unretrieved dead from both sides were evident only by the mounding of the snow above their still forms.

16

The long night had passed, bringing renewed fighting in the morning. With the fighting came an additional menace from the soldiers. On that second day of battle they were firing from their big gun. Its bursting shells fell far short of the camp until the soldiers, by some adjustment, gained accuracy with the weapon.

For the rest of the day there was no respite from the terror that the big gun inflicted as its random shells exploded into the trenches where the noncombatants were huddled.

The day was wild and stormy. The swirling snow and the smoke of the firing made the air thick, and it lessened accuracy on both sides.

The long knives had strengthened their siege line, and they fought on relentlessly until noon, when an officer raised a white flag from behind some sheltering rocks.

Takseen was slow to realize its significance, slow even to see it against the whiteness that was everywhere. Despair was so widespread throughout the Nez Perce camp that the people dared not hope the flag signified an end to the hostilities.

With the white flag, the shooting ceased and for a time

the heavy artillery was silenced, giving relief from the serious damage it had inflicted all throughout the morning.

"What's the meaning of this?" Takseen inquired of her brother.

"Wait and see, my sister," Yellow Moccasin responded wearily. "We must never trust the whites."

The soldiers disappeared from view and for a while silence continued, but after only a brief interval the firing resumed.

"That was not a flag of peace," Yellow Moccasin told his sister. There was bitterness in his voice. "They only ceased fire long enough to fill their stomachs. Now they are ready to fight again."

There was shooting the rest of the day until the invisible sun again set behind the storm clouds. There was deeper cold, more snow, with the coming darkness.

Takseen slept intermittently through the night, leaning against the frigid earthen walls of the main shelter pit.

The third morning of the battle came, but none were killed. The bullets spent themselves in the icy air, as if the continued battle were merely a game.

The day before, an old woman and a child of twelve snows had been killed by a shell that exploded in a trench and caved in the walls. Three other women were buried, but they were pulled from the earth with no serious injuries. On the third morning the heavy artillery was silent. No more shells fell into the trenches that sheltered the helpless old ones, women, and children.

A sense of deep despair accompanied the desultory firing. The feeling was unbroken until midafternoon. In the back of her mind Takseen, like the others, nursed a secret hope for reinforcements. Joseph had sent runners to carry word concerning their plight to Sitting Bull's Sioux warriors in the Old Woman's country. The Nez Perce still held out a faint hope of help from their red brothers to the north.

It was that thought that sprang to mind when a joyful shout rang out from the rifle pits. Takseen lifted her head above the enclosure and peered into the swirling storm. There were dark shapes on the horizon. Reinforcements!

"Sitting Bull's warriors!" a triumphant voice shouted.

The snow-covered forms moved closer while the defenders squinted into the storm, their hearts pounding. Then hope was dashed from the hearts of the people. Yellow Moccasin's voice went flat. "They are only buffalo. Look how the snow clings to their thick hides."

Takseen felt the flicker of hope die within her breast and she settled back against the trench wall. She tried to shut out the hunger pains that clutched at her stomach. For two days she had eaten nothing, and she felt herself growing weaker, more vulnerable to the cold that prodded and seeped into even the most sheltered recesses of the pits.

"Soon I will be like the old ones, huddled in their blankets with death in their eyes," she thought. "I must start moving." Within the shelter of the trench she began exercising her numbed extremities.

There had been no shooting for some time and she risked standing up to stretch her cramped muscles. Then, on the bluff to the south she saw a scene enacted so quickly she scarcely realized what had happened. A warrior stood, imprudently exposed to the enemy, in order to observe something in the distance. "Could he see a courier from the Sioux?" she wondered anxiously. In the next moment he was felled by a shot in the forehead. The brave lay dead upon the ground before Takseen could discover his identity.

Takseen motioned Yellow Moccasin to her side. "That was Looking Glass," Yellow Moccasin told her dully. Another chief, the fifth since the battle had begun, lay dead upon the snow-covered plains of Tsanim Alikos Pah.

The witnesses spread the word, and the gloom that en-

veloped the beleaguered defenders was as thick as the storm
that raged above their heads.

So it was that when the white flag was again raised on
that third day of battle, the Indians responded with little
feeling, having no trust in the whites and no hope for their
own salvation.

Takseen watched as a messenger from "Bear Coat" Miles's
camp crossed over to the Indian side. He conferred with a
small group of warriors through an interpreter and a parley
was arranged.

Two white soldiers spread a bison robe at a halfway point
between the siege line and the Indian camp. Joseph, with two
of his trusted warriors, went unarmed to the designated spot
to meet with Bear Coat and his advisers.

As it had been at Lolo Pass, the conference achieved
nothing. Before very long Joseph shook his head sadly and
turned on his heel to return to camp.

Then a stunned exclamation arose from the lips of the
watchers. Miles's advisers laid hands on Joseph and led him
back to their camp. The Indians strongly distrusted the
Colonel's motives for detaining the chief, and from the gullies
the warriors raised their rifles in protest. They prudently
withheld their fire, however, for to shoot would only jeopard-
ize Joseph's life.

They had their opportunity to retaliate when an officer,
sent by Miles to reconnoiter the Indian camp, rode too close
to its perimeter. One of Chief White Bird's warriors, by the
name of Yellow Bull, seized the bridle reins of the black
horse and pulled its rider from the saddle.

Takseen was close enough to see that the young man
showed no fear. He was dressed in a yellow coat of some
material that kept the wetness from him and he appeared

well fed and rested. Takseen could not help but contrast his appearance with the Indian warriors' whose gaunt faces reflected weariness, hunger, and cold. Their clothing, some of it, was shredded by bullets, and the light had gone from their eyes.

Chuslum Hihhih shouted, "I want to kill this soldier!" but Yellow Bull and the others restrained him.

They took the officer to the main shelter pit, and as night approached, his guards shared a small supper and some water with him. Yellow Bull and another warrior continued the watch to protect him from Chuslum Hihhih or any others who would hurt him. That soldier was their insurance that Joseph would be unharmed. During the night they gave him a buffalo robe for a bed.

Takseen wondered if Joseph was being treated with equal kindness. She spent the night in the shelter pit beside Springtime. Joseph's wife did not sleep. For three days neither she nor Takseen had tasted food, and Joseph's baby daughter was failing badly.

"Let me hold the child," Takseen offered halfway through the night. "You must rest. Surely tomorrow the white soldiers will offer us Joseph's freedom in exchange for the officer-prisoner we hold."

Springtime nodded. "I hope you're right. I fear for his life." She handed the listless child to Takseen, who held the baby close within her own blankets. The little one made an attempt to cry and beat her fists weakly against the coverings, but finally slept. Takseen tried to put the memories from her mind of her own infant sister, but the picture persisted of the child lying helplessly on her mother's breast, waving her shattered arm back and forth that infamous day at the Big Hole. In a moment of helpless rage she let the tears fall and squeezed the sleeping babe closely against her, thinking, "What will become of this child? What will become of my people?"

The fourth morning of the battle dawned. The cold and hunger were taking their toll on the noncombatants; there was little movement within camp.

The captured officer was allowed to walk about within a narrow radius of the shelter pit. The leaders gave orders that he should not be harmed.

Takseen left her shelter briefly to obtain water for herself and for Joseph's wife. She was filling a container when Yellow Bull called out to her.

"Bring this man water for drinking."

Takseen did as she was bidden. The officer took a long drink and handed back the vessel.

"Thank you," he said in his own tongue, but Takseen could read both gratitude and pity in his eyes, and she understood what he had said. She could not smile, for he represented the annihilation of everything she had ever loved; she merely nodded curtly and started to leave. The strong-looking young man conferred with Yellow Bull by means of signs.

Takseen was refilling her water container when Yellow Bull inquired, "Is your brother nearby? This officer wishes to send a message to his camp. Yellow Moccasin can relay it."

"I'll get him."

She found her brother among the horses, the gaunt handful that were left. She relayed Yellow Bull's message and followed her brother in order to watch from a respectable distance. There had been no shooting that day, and she felt no fear as she stood on the snow-packed earth, glad to be above ground.

The young soldier handed a written message first to a

Nez Perce who knew English. The Indian read aloud so that the others could hear what was written.

"I had a good supper and a good bed, plenty of blankets. This morning I had a good breakfast. I am treated like I was at home. I hope you are treating Chief Joseph as I am treated."

The warriors nodded their approval and gave the message to Yellow Moccasin to carry across to the other camp.

Takseen was apprehensive for her brother's safety while he was gone. The minutes seemed long, but when he returned he brought with him good news; Bear Coat was willing to make an exchange.

"You come across to us. When you get here Chief Joseph can go," the return message read.

Before the warriors could make a decision, Yellow Moccasin told them what he had seen in the white soldiers' camp. "Chief Joseph hasn't been treated kindly. He was hobbled and rolled in blankets and given no food."

"Then we can't trust them to return our chief safely," said Yellow Bull. "Take back another message to Bear Coat. Tell him that if he is speaking true, he'll bring Joseph halfway, to the same ground where we met before. Then we'll return their officer."

Yellow Moccasin made his way across the intervening prairie once again. That time, after a brief interval, Takseen saw a white flag go up. A party of escorts brought Joseph to the midway point and again spread a buffalo robe on the ground. The few remaining chiefs in the Indian camp and a handful of older warriors met them with the white prisoner.

Takseen watched them shake hands and each return across the drifted snow to their respective sides.

Springtime stood beside her, and as the two young women watched in the freezing air, Takseen could sense the relief Springtime felt at the safe return of her husband.

Yet his return did not signify any change in the status of the siege. He spoke to the headmen, and Takseen heard his words with a heavy heart.

"I was hobbled in the soldier camp. I was not treated right. We must fight more. The war is not quit!"

The white flag came down and the warriors began exchanging shots with the soldiers. The Indians expected an eventual charge, and they rationed their ammunition accordingly.

The remainder of the day and still another stormy night passed heavily while the warriors kept watch for an enemy charge throughout the long night.

17

The fifth morning dawned, but the sun did not show itself. Again the big gun started up, lobbing shells into the trenches where the noncombatants were sheltered.

"Surely Bear Coat knows there are only women and children in these pits," Takseen worried aloud to Yellow Moccasin. "His spy was in our camp for nearly a full day. We even let him walk about."

"You're right, sister. He must have told them there are no fighting men in this part of camp. . . ."

His sentence was cut short by a tremendous explosion close by. The sides of the pit caved in and a shrill scream was muffled by falling earth. Takseen and Yellow Moccasin scrambled to the place. Other hands joined in the task of removing the dirt and debris that half-buried an old woman. They gently brushed the dirt from her face and found that she was still breathing.

Takseen brought water and washed the dirt from the old one's face and arms, patting her wrinkled skin dry to ward off the cold. There was only a blank stare in return for the spare blanket that Takseen wrapped her in. Takseen was beyond words except for small murmurs of comfort to the confused old woman; in her heart she felt toward the white man a bitterness that deadened all her feelings.

She realized that the state of siege could not go on much longer. Toward nightfall the end was clearly coming; it was on that fifth day of battle that General Howard arrived with two scouts. His reinforcements were not far behind.

That evening Howard's scouts approached the camp waving a white flag. Takseen joined the shivering people who huddled together to hear their message. When she saw their faces, Takseen gave a start of recognition. The pair were Nez Perce, one of whom had a daughter in Joseph's camp.

The first one, whom she knew as Captain John, greeted those ragged survivors who were strong enough to leave the shelter pits.

"All my brothers, I am glad to see you alive this day! We have traveled far to find you. We are glad to hear you want no more war."

There was a stir of anger among the listeners. Chuslum Hihhih, who had been anxious to kill the white hostage earlier, shouted angrily, "Let us shoot these traitors!" He was again restrained by strong hands.

Then Old George took up the greeting. It was he who had a daughter among Takseen's people.

"We have come far from home. You now see many soldiers lying down side by side. We see Indians, too, lying dead. I am glad today to be shaking hands. We are not all mad. We all think of Chief Joseph and these other brothers. We see your sons and relations lying dead, but we are glad to shake hands with you today. I am glad to catch up with you and find my daughter, too, alive."

By turns they assured Chiefs Joseph and White Bird that Colonel Miles was an honorable man whom they could trust. Through their assurances they laid the groundwork for a meeting of the leaders.

When the two had returned to the soldier camp, Joseph and White Bird retired to hold council with the warriors.

Takseen listened to the rise and fall of voices. She gathered that White Bird continued to oppose surrender, but he wouldn't force his views upon Joseph. Tribal law did not require unanimity for a decision; the chiefs could decide separately for their bands.

So it was that Joseph looked around at the starving, shivering people he had led so great a distance. He had shared in the task of battle plans with the other chiefs, but he had singly carried the burden of protector of the people throughout the long journey. It was for their welfare that he made his final decision. He looked once more at the hungry faces and thin bodies; some did not even have blankets as they stood about, anticipating his decision. The cries of hunger from the little ones fell upon his ears.

"It is for them that I am going to surrender," he said simply, gesturing toward the shelter pits from which the crying issued. "When we spoke before, Colonel Miles told me in plain words, 'If you will come out and give up your arms, I will spare your lives and send you back to the reservation.' With that promise in mind, I will speak to him now."

The two Nez Perce from the soldier camp had returned under protection of the white flag. They were anxious for a decision to take to Miles and Howard.

"Tell them we will quit the war," Joseph said with finality. His face was sad, but in it Takseen could see the pride in his people for having fought so long and well.

Joseph stood tall as he addressed himself to the messengers. His blanket and moccasin leggings were tattered in more than a dozen places from bullet holes; they spoke vividly of the suffering he had endured throughout the long ordeal. More than that, he symbolized the suffering of all the people. There was complete silence as the waiting Nez Perce listened for the words he would send to Miles and Howard. There was infinite sadness in Joseph's eyes as he began quietly. The stinging wind that swept across the plains carried his words to his followers.

"Tell General Howard I know his heart. What he told me before I have in my heart. I am tired of fighting. Our chiefs are killed. Looking Glass is dead. The old men are all killed. It is the young men who say yes or no. He who led the young men is dead. It is cold and we have no blankets. The little children are freezing to death. My people, some of them, have run away to the hills and have no blankets, no food; no one knows where they are, perhaps freezing to death. I want time to look for my children and see how many of them I can fiind. Maybe I shall find them among the dead. Hear me, my chiefs; I am tired; my heart is sick and sad. From where the sun now stands, I will fight no more forever."

Captain John's eyes were filled with tears as he and Old George turned from the cluster of homeless ones, their tribal brothers who silently ringed the snow-covered battlefield with a solemn expression of both pride and humility on their faces.

Upon receiving the message, General O. O. Howard and Colonel Nelson Miles, along with three officers and their interpreter, Ad Chapman, gathered upon the parley ground to await formal surrender.

In the Indian camp there were mixed feelings. Takseen felt primarily an overwhelming sadness.

"We haven't lost this battle, sister," Yellow Moccasin told her. "It was a draw."

"It is past time to talk of wins and losses," Takseen answered sharply. "I would not call this winning," and she gestured toward the ragged remnants of the Nez Perce bands. "I can't even call it a draw. Nothing was ever even about this war." She touched the moss agate at her breast and tenderly ran a finger over its smooth surface. "For my part, I have lost everything but my own life and yours."

"Then we must stand together, sister." Yellow Moccasin reached out and touched his sister's shoulder. For a moment they looked deeply into one another's eyes. The boy had grown taller than Takseen in the past months, and she took great comfort in his presence when he put his arms around her.

"You'll feel better when you've eaten. There will be fires tonight, and hot food." He clumsily wiped a tear from Takseen's cheek.

Her tears subsided, but the bitterness within her caused her heart to ache. "Is it for this that we journeyed all these miles, that we fought so many battles—to be finally sent to the place we fought to avoid?"

"Is there so much hatred then in your heart?"

"I should not call it hate. Joseph does not hate. He only loves." Takseen looked toward the chief, who was shielding his eyes from the stinging snow as he gazed into the distance. She shook her head in sudden realization. "This whole war was a mistake. It shouldn't have happened, but it did; and we did what we had to, just as the soldiers did their job. Surely they have been stung by death just as we." Takseen struck her breast in frustration. "I wish my heart could feel warmth again. I cannot live with this hate. I cannot live with this bitterness. What has happened to me, my brother?"

"Things will be better with time. That is what the old ones say, and I believe it must be true." He put his arm around Takseen's thin shoulders once again and pointed toward the parley ground.

"Look, the soldier chiefs are waiting, and Joseph is mounting his horse."

Joseph rode alone. His head was bowed and his thick

braids hung down upon his gray woolen shawl. The shawl and his buckskin leggings were pierced with bullet holes; Takseen could tell from that distance how tattered they were. Joseph rode clasping the saddle pommel, his rifle across his knees. He never looked aside as he ascended the hill to the waiting soldier chiefs.

When he drew near the officers, he swung off his horse. He stood straight as he flung out his arm full length, offering his rifle to General Howard.

Howard generously motioned his arm aside, allowing Miles to accept the token of surrender. Then the officers all shook hands with Joseph. They had prepared a tent for the Nez Perce chief and they led him toward it.

The unarmed warriors who had followed on foot stayed in the white camp, waiting for Joseph to emerge from the tent.

It was over. With heavy heart Takseen began searching through the packed snow for buffalo chips and branches. At least they would have a warm fire that night.

Joseph returned within the hour. He dismounted at the edge of camp and left his horse with a warrior. He walked through the village, urging the people from the coulees, telling them to give up their arms.

"No more battles. No more blood. That is what Bear Coat said to me. We will pass the winter at Fort Keogh and in the spring return to Lapwai. That is his promise."

The people responded to his urgings, and one by one or in small groups they straggled up the hill to surrender their weapons. When they returned they came with generous sacks of flour and portions of meat. Colonel Miles was unselfish with the food and the little boys and girls loved him for that. For the little ones, the war would soon be miraculously forgotten.

While the survivors left and returned, Takseen pondered

the decision that she couldn't make alone. "What are you going to do, my brother?"

Yellow Moccasin too showed indecision in his handsome young face. "White Bird did not surrender. He will be escaping soon under cover of darkness with many of his band. They say they will flee to Canada."

"Do we have that choice?" Takseen wondered.

"Would you desert Joseph?" he asked her.

"In my heart I could not join with White Bird. Yet I have little faith in the promises of the white men. What if we aren't allowed to returned to Idaho in the spring? Perhaps the authorities will send us far away. What then?"

"We cannot know for certain."

"We said before, my brother, we've lost everything—our mother and father, our sister, our good friends, my betrothed. . . ." Her voice trailed off and she again fingered the amulet. "I have a strong feeling," Takseen continued softly. "You must believe me when I say that things will not be as they are promised if we surrender."

"Then let's flee," Yellow Moccasin decided for her.

"With White Bird's people?"

"No. Just us. We can slip past the pickets when darkness comes. We shall winter with the Sioux or the Assiniboins. When spring comes, we can make our way back to Idaho. Then we'll know if the soldier chiefs were speaking straight."

"Is it honorable to desert Joseph now?"

"It's a risk either way. We have fought long and hard for our freedom. Yes, it is honorable to seek freedom."

Throughout the day small groups continued to return from the soldier camp. The morale improved a great deal as the people had an opportunity to warm themselves and fill their stomachs. Those who had been in the other camp reported that the soldiers were occupied with stacking the surrendered firearms and burying their dead. In addition to caring for their own wounded, the soldiers were generous in treating the wounds of their prisoners.

With so much activity, it was not difficult for Takseen to prepare for escape. Yellow Moccasin hand-picked four ponies that remained from Lone Coyote's once vast herd. They were thin and bone-weary, but they were not sick or lame as most of the others were. The boy hid the animals in a coulee. In that place Takseen assembled the things they would need. There was meat from the soldier camp that Springtime had shared with her. Only one spare blanket for each of them remained. She loaded the pack ponies, discarding some of the possessions she had carried so far. She took a long look at the soiled, blood-stained garment that was to have been her bridal outfit and tenderly pushed it to the bottom of the pack. It would be important to travel lightly, but some things were too precious to give up.

By nightfall Colonel Miles had doubled the number of pickets on guard around the camp. They were watchful for any attempts to escape. Nevertheless, when the night had advanced sufficiently, Chief White Bird and more than twenty of his people slipped out of camp. They were aided by a swirling storm that swept down through the darkness, rendering them nearly invisible. Takseen was aware of their leaving and in her heart she wished them well. She listened for the report of a rifle, but there was none as the people stole silently past the pickets.

"Are you ready, sister?" Yellow Moccasin asked her softly when White Bird's people had had a short start.

"Yes." Takseen's heart was pounding. They would be in grave danger; if they were discovered they would doubtless be pursued and shot down. It was said that the hundred or so of White Bird's people who had escaped on the first day of the siege were still being sought by a detachment of Bear Coat's men.

"Are you frightened, sister?" Yellow Moccasin touched her shoulder and looked into her black eyes.

She turned her head from his direct gaze. "A little," she admitted softly. "I know deep within me that to surrender would mean more suffering and death. I'll willingly take my chances to the north. Let's be off."

Yellow Moccasin picked up the reins of her pack pony and handed them to her. "I know you have looked into your heart, my sister, and your spirit has spoken the truth to you." He gave a small hopeful smile. "We shall make our own way from this day forward. The soldiers can have neither our bodies nor our spirits."

In spite of the optimism, his reference brought a fleeting sense of despair to Takseen. "Promise me, brother, that when it's safe to return, we shall look for the place where we left the bones of our loved ones. I'd like to go back just one more time." There were tears in her eyes. "Later, when I can better bear to remember."

"It is done," he answered softly. "Let's go now."

They followed the winding course of the coulee. It was a path to freedom as it wound about the camp and out toward the watchful guard. It sheltered them from discovery and from the winds that gusted overheard, carrying great clouds of snow.

Yellow Moccasin and Takseen were soon beyond the flickering of the campfires. Only an occasional sound drifted brokenly on the wind, but the sense of it was scattered by the storm. Beyond the main part of camp the snow within the coulee was no longer packed by wear. In places it was drifted so that Yellow Moccasin had to break a trail with his body before the ponies would move.

There was only a vast darkness ahead and no starlight to guide them. Yellow Moccasin held up his arm and warned Takseen to stop. They muffled their horses' heads with their arms for a moment and listened. She heard what had stopped her brother; there was a crunch of boots on the fresh snow. They ceased even to breathe as the steps came closer. The sentinel approached the edge of the coulee, then stopped. For a brief moment Takseen could see his shape dimly etched against the blackness of the night. She dared not breathe. The soldier peered along the length of the crevice, but his sight was blinded by the swirling snow. Then he turned and his boots crunched across the snow back toward camp.

Wordlessly the two struggled through the drifts until the coulee came to an end. They knew their position roughly from the reconnoitering Yellow Moccasin had done earlier. By following the base of a northerly ridge, they could get a safe distance from camp before dawn, and the snow would be drifted less in its lee. With the morning light they could readjust their route.

Takseen turned for a last look. There had been few farewells in the camp. She had confided only in Springtime that she was leaving. She said a silent farewell in her heart to the camp that lay behind them, its fires showing intermittently through the gusts of snow.

Then she swung into her saddle and picked up the reins of the pack pony. Drawing her blanket more tightly about her shoulders she leaned into the wind and nudged her pony's ribs.

Into the blackness and cold, Takseen and Yellow Moccasin made their way, toward the north where lay the Old Woman's country and freedom.

18

Matt grasped Katy's shoulders and shook her. She had wailed the death song with trembling voice for many minutes. Her expression had changed entirely, so that she resembled for that interval the young girl of the journal who had sorrowed there a hundred years earlier. Katy's black hair hung in thick braids on her shoulders, and her large eyes, although blue and not black, expressed the infinite sadness of her tribal heritage.

The sky was still rolling with oily black clouds, but the wind and rain remained poised as if waiting. Then, as her trembling voice at last subsided, the keening of the wind began again, picking up the dreadful wail.

"Katy!" Matt said shaking her gently. "For God's sake, please come out of it!" He was badly frightened by her appearance. Her features were slowly regaining familiarity, but he could not fathom the look in her eyes. She was physically present, yet she was not of this world. Katy had slipped into a deep trance-like state and she moved from his grasp, squatting on her heels, rocking back and forth with her arms folded across her chest.

"Shall I take you back to the truck until the storm

passes?" Matt needn't have asked the question. She continued rocking, locked within her own world as if possessed, and she refused the hand he offered to help her up.

Matt gently laid a light coat about her shoulders. They would have to weather out the storm, for there was only one thing that would free Katy from her possessed state.

He withdrew the folding shovel from his satchel and gently probed the earth with it. He would have to work carefully, yet quickly, before darkness overtook them. There were perhaps two or three hours left before sunset.

The wind ceased its violent gusting and began blowing a steady course across the plain. Katy sat on her heels, the coat around her shoulders, but she took no notice of the violent precursor of the storm.

The graves were shallow and Matt soon knew he had found something. With his hands he brushed away the dirt from the object he had found. He looked at his discovery with tenderness but refrained from lifting it from the earth. It was a small skull, no bigger than an infant's—Takseen's baby sister. It was not for him to disrupt the long sleep of those innocents in the bosom of their earth mother. He carefully replaced the sod above the skull of the little one.

The grave he sought surely would be close by. He continued his probe, that time on the far side of the lofty pine. The grave again was shallow, but the earth was hard. It would remain so only a short while longer, however, for the first large drops were falling upon the thirsty earth. Then the rain came in sheets, driven before the moaning wind. The dust turned to mud beneath his shovel. Working quickly Matt loosened the top layer of earth, then used his hands to move aside the wet soil. That grave was as shallow as the others, but the bones he exposed lay in disorder. Not only the Indians and the marauding animals had disturbed them, but the root system of the tree had gradually destroyed portions of the skeleton.

Katy, still rocking gently, stared at Matt as he reached

down to touch the skull he had fully exposed. He laid his hand on the flattened portion where only wisps of long black hair remained. The signs of scalping were obvious, but as his hand made contact with the cranium, a sudden vibration startled him. He looked to the top of the hill directly overhead where a rocky outcrop seemed to be a source of an intense vibration, a zinging sound. His sense of other-worldliness almost got the better of him, and he shook his head in wonderment. Then the rocks atop the hillside joined in the humming. Suddenly, with an instantaneous explosive sound, a bolt of lightning slammed into the rocky outcrop that jutted from the ridge.

After the initial shock had passed, Matt felt a sense of relief; it was not a supernatural phenomenon after all. On other occasions he had been atop a ridge and experienced the vibrating noise of the rocks just before lightning struck. The sense of unreality had nearly caused him to put a different interpretation to the occurrence.

The blinding white flash and the simultaneous explosive sound of thunder left the smell of ozone in the air. Matt looked to Katy to see if she was okay, and was startled to see the change in her. The thunderous crash had jolted her into motion.

She stood and spread her lightweight coat upon the ground. She spoke in a solemn voice, both like and unlike Katy's.

"This is not enough," she said, gesturing toward the open grave where Matt had started to align the bones. "Many spirits. Some are at peace, but others . . . The place is evil." She drew closer but would not touch the bones. "Lay them there," she said pointing to her coat.

"We can't remove them, little one," Matt told her gently, clasping her shoulders and looking deep into her eyes. "Trust me. I'll replace the bones. We'll restore peace to the spirit of Buffalo Robe."

"This is not enough, I tell you. He cannot rest in this

evil place." The rain ran in rivulets down her face as she squeezed Matt's hand, begging him. "To the Wallowa. We must return him to the Winding Water. Then we'll all find peace."

Matt considered the request. There was no point in arguing with Katy. She was probably not even totally aware of what was happening. However, when he had sought permission from the information officer to search for the graves, he had agreed not to disturb or remove any artifacts.

Yet something within him urged him to do as she said. That place, the Big Hole National Battlefield, belonged to the people of the United States; yet somehow, more importantly, the bones of Buffalo Robe belonged to their earth mother. That they should be removed to a more suitable resting place seemed morally right. Restoration of peace to Buffalo Robe's soul seemed even more basic than preserving that portion of the site for the enjoyment of tourists.

With that justification in mind, Matt cast an anxious eye toward the visitor center. The electrical power was still off.

The storm raged in all its fury while Matt extricated the remaining bones from the earth. The skeleton was clearly incomplete and the arms and leg bones were damaged. The skull and the smaller bones he laid within the satchel, but he had to conceal the longer ones within Katy's coat. He told her to put it on, then placed the long bones vertically beneath it. She clutched the edges of the coat together, shuddering as they touched the wet fabric of her shirt. If she walked hunched into the wind with her arms clasped around her, the deception would probably work when they passed the information center.

Matt finished his task by replacing the soil and smoothing it down. He scattered leaves and pine needles across the surface, then marked the site of Buffalo Robe's grave with a boulder. He placed a smaller rock atop the grave of the women and the infant.

Satisfied with the job, he looked at Katy. The task,

strangely enough, had not been a grisly one. Even though it had dredged up such painful memories of the past, there was a sense of spiritual fulfillment about it.

Nevertheless, Katy, in her confusion of roles, displayed reluctance to handle the bones because she attached such significance to the spirit they represented. She clearly felt a restless presence amidst the graves of the innocent dead.

"Is everything all right?" Matt asked her.

She nodded.

"Let's go then. When we approach the visitor center, I'll give you the satchel. Keep on going until you're in the truck," Matt instructed her. "I'll check and see if anyone is still inside."

In the fury of the storm they made their way out of the protecting ravine and crossed the shallow river. There was no need to remove their shoes.

Matt and Katy felt the full force of the lashing wind and rain when they left the shelter of the ravine and crossed into open prairie They leaned into the wind and followed the trail back to the visitor center. Just before ascending the small rise that would put them in full view of anyone watching, Matt transferred the satchel to Katy's possession.

When they drew abreast of the building, she kept walking as he had instructed while he went inside the main entrance.

It was dark within the room, but a flashlight beam found him.

"Mr. Moss?"

"Yes."

"I waited around for you. Everyone else has gone home." It was the same employee from whom Matt had obtained permission to search the battlefield. "I was worried about you two. You were gone such a long time."

"Well, sir, we thought we could wait out the storm, but we finally gave up." Matt gestured apologetically to his dripping clothes.

"Did you find the place you were looking for?"

"Yes, I'm almost positive. I marked the graves with some rocks, if you want to check." Matt described the location more fully. "I would guess the family journals which we were relying on to find the graves must have been accurate. I'm quite certain the two places we marked were the spots where two women and an infant and a warrior were buried on the day of the Big Hole Massacre."

The officer gave Matt a suspicious look. "Why are you so certain? I trust you didn't disturb anything. By the way, the young lady was carrying a satchel. I don't mean to imply anything unpleasant, but would you mind if I searched its contents?"

"I certainly would mind," Matt told him emphatically. He hated to be forced into a position of lying, but he was dealing with a person who apparently went by the books and would never release the bones, even if he wanted to.

"The young lady had her camera equipment and tripod in the satchel, also the journals that we spoke of. If you search the bag it will badly upset her. This experience has been emotionally upsetting for her, and she is quite distraught at the moment."

The official seemed perplexed. "In that case I'll probably have to take your word for it."

"Perhaps you'll understand better if I tell you that she has recently followed portions of Chief Joseph's line of retreat. For the past few days she has litrally been reliving the past, and today she saw the place where her great-great-grandmother and her great-grandmother's betrothed were interred. The day of the Big Hole battle was to have been the wedding day of her great-grandmother. I'm sure you understand the inherent tragedy in the situation, and you can see why she's upset."

Matt held out his hand to the uniformed young man. The fellow shook his head, saying, "I must say, this has all

been highly irregular. Nevertheless, I appreciate the information you added to our knowledge of the battlefield. If we
can authenticate your findings, we'll include them in the proposed trail-guide brochure of the massacre area. I'll be in
touch with you."

Matt inwardly flinched. Authentication meant digging
into the grave sites. That single afternoon's activities could
eventually cost him his job, but he was convinced that he and
Katy were right in what they were doing; it was right for
both of them as well as for the memory of Buffalo Robe.

"Thanks for your help, and for your understanding,"
Matt said as he left.

Back in the pickup he found Katy in the same disoriented
state he had come to expect. The satchel and the bundled
raincoat lay in the seat beside her.

"We must leave this place of evil forever," she stated in
that curious voice that was not entirely her own.

The storm had scattered to the east and only a gentle rain
fell steadily against the windshield. The slap of the wipers
was the only sound as Matt drove through the early darkness
to the junction with the highway that led north through the
Bitterroot Valley. There was no way they could cross that
night into the Oregon country that was the homeland of
Joseph's Wallamwatkins, but he was intent on covering at
least half the distance.

The darkness was a blessing, for it blotted the scenery of
the valley from view. They were following Joseph's trek in
reverse, and Katy's state was serious enough that Matt wanted
to free her from any more unpleasant associations. He was
happy when she dozed at last, and some of his tension lifted.
They had by then crossed the Lolo Pass and dropped into
Idaho.

They left the storm to the south and a nearly full moon
broke through the clouds. Its pale light reflected off the rush-

ing waters of the Lochsa River. The water was low, but the sight of the river rushing between the silvered slopes never failed to stir him with its primitive beauty. In many ways Matt felt a kinship for that part of the country as strong as Katy's. Just as he had grown attached to the old cabin site where he had first met Katy, he felt a similar closeness, like a sharp intake of recognition, every time he followed the Lolo Trail.

With the brightness the moonlight afforded, Matt felt refreshed and continued driving until he'd covered nearly a hundred more miles of wilderness. Along the edge of the road his headlights picked up an occasional deer or raccoon. Once a large furry animal with a bushy tail paused to stare into the oncoming headlights before disappearing into the brush.

He came at last, two hours past midnight, to a cluster of cabins for rent. He recognized the place and had stayed there previously. He crossed the bridge over the Lochsa, a few yards from where it joined the Selway to form the middle fork of the Clearwater. It was a beautiful junction where the two valleys came together and he was happy in anticipation of spending a night in a log cabin beside the rushing waters.

There was one cabin still free and he registered for it.

"Katy," he said softly, shaking her shoulder, "we're stopping now." Her dozing had slipped into deeper sleep and he couldn't awaken her. Instead, he unlocked the cabin door and carried her to the back room, where a log partition separated it from the rest of the cabin. He laid her on the bed. Her clothing had dried by then and it stuck to her in mud-caked streaks. Since he was still unable to awaken her, he awkwardly pulled the sheet and a plaid wool blanket over her and set her suitcase by the foot of the bed. She stirred momentarily and blinked a time or two.

"Just rest, little one. It's very late. Tomorrow we can finish our task. Tomorrow you'll be well again."

She nodded as if she understood. "Please bring the satchel in, and the other too." She couldn't call it by name. "Lay them in the other room." Then she slipped back to sleep.

Matt did as she asked. After a quick shower he had no trouble falling asleep; but in his sleep, the presence of the bones of the warrior Buffalo Robe affected the course of his dreams. He saw himself standing on a grassy ridge overlooking a blue mountain lake. On the shore were the two he had come to know through the experiences of the past few weeks. The pair, Takseen and Buffalo Robe, were dressed in their soft leather wedding clothes. Gone were the stains of blood the smudges of dirt and gunpowder. The clothes were new and clean and worn as they were intended to be worn. Takseen's brilliant black eyes were lit with an expression of love as she looked at her handsome warrior. They turned from him then, and hand in hand gazed across the water. It was a bright sunny day and the reflections glinting on the water were painfully brilliant. As he watched, the radiance of the sun grew even brighter, pulsating rhythmically, growing, spreading, finally consuming the pair in its fiery rays.

The dream ended, and with it came a sense of well-being that Matt had not experienced for a long time. "If dreaming is wish fulfillment," he thought to himself, "then we will soon have resolved forever the tragedy of Takseen and Buffalo Robe."

Through his half-awake reflections he heard the sound of water running. In his sleepy state it was hard to separate it from the sounds of the water that tumbled over boulders just outside his window. He slipped back into sleep, only to be awakened again by a soft fragrance and a gentle hand on his shoulder.

When he opened his eyes, Matt saw Katy standing above him. She had awakened and showered, and her black hair hung loose and clean and shining dark against the white of her soft flannel gown. The light fragrance of her caused Matt to long to take her in his arms.

"Please hold me," she said quietly in a child's voice. "I'm frightened."

Matt drew her down beside him and held her close. The physical nearness of her was almost more than he could bear, yet there was no question of making love to her. She was like a hypnotized child. Moreover, he had never affirmed his love for her, nor she to him. Later, perhaps . . .

The night passed too quickly. Matt took great comfort from the warmth of the flannel-clad body curled beside him, and the radiant vision of his dream had left him with a sense of peace. He held Katy close until dawn, thinking his silent thoughts. Then he too slept.

It was close to 10 A.M when a sharp knocking awakened him. He pulled on his trousers and begrudgingly walked to the door, calling, "Yes, who is it?" There was no answer and he opened the door just a crack in deference to Katy, who was still sleeping soundly.

"Richard!" Matt was unable to keep the surprise from his voice.

"Where is she?" Richard said roughly, pushing Matt aside. He entered the cabin and took in the rumpled bed and the sleeping form, and his anger was expressed in a visible shaking as he clenched his fist and glared at Matt.

"Katy," he said loudly, shaking the sleeping girl. "If he's touched you, I'll file charges. Rape, kidnapping—whatever it takes to put him away." He looked wildly at Matt, then turned Katy over and shook her again. "Hey, what's wrong with her anyway? Is she drugged?"

The wild look was replaced by fear when Richard saw how inert Katy remained as she stared up at him uncomprehendingly.

"Richard, you better come outside," Matt said quietly.

"Well, it looks like you've got a lot of explaining to do." Richard followed Matt out the door. The rise and fall of angry voices came to Katy as she lay there, unable to recognize Richard or to understand the significance of the argument.

When Matt re-entered the cabin he was alone. There was a peeling of tires and the sound of gravel flying as Richard departed.

Katy had dressed by then, and she looked toward Matt with a puzzled expression. Matt attempted an explanation.

"Richard talked to your mother in Spokane Wednesday. He forced her to disclose our destination and he's been following us since yesterday." Matt passed his hand across his brow. "Whew. I wasn't exactly expecting him this morning." He looked to Katy for a reaction, but there was none. She had no questions concerning the surprise appearance of her fiancé, and Matt concluded that her trancelike state was so deep that there was no use in making further explanation.

He went to the door and returned with a brown box tied with string. "Your mother sent this with Richard for you. She thought it might help, whatever it is. She begged Richard to be gentle and tried to prepare him—she told him all you've been through."

Katy didn't so much as hold out her hand to receive the package, so Matt, with a shrug of his shoulders, set the box on the bed.

"There's only one thing you want, isn't there, little one?" He put his arms around her gently. "We'll finish the task we set out to accomplish. Then whatever it is that has such a hold on you can let go and set us all free. You'll see."

He released her and set about the business of packing their few belongings. Katy had retreated so deeply into her shell that even Matt had doubts about the wisdom of his plan. Would anything they did release the terrible hold on Katy's mind? He dared not show his waning confidence to Katy. The peaceful feeling of the early morning fled and tension returned full force.

19

Matt looked down on the lake below him. It lay shimmering and unreal in the silvered light of the full moon. Katy stood beside him, and for a moment he drew his arm more tightly around her waist, trying to dispel his sense of unreality by reassuring himself of her physical presence.

She was real and she was silent, but her entranced state was imbued with a sense of hopeful urgency, though she had said little all day.

For one sweet moment Matt thought about that early morning. Katy, peaceful in sleep, had looked infinitely beautiful as he had held her slumbering form. He tried not to think about the shattering of his early-morning idyll.

He remembered her lack of comprehension of the entire incident. Her sense of reality seemed still trapped in a far-off corner of her mind. She clearly was not yet released from the hold that the bones of Buffalo Robe held over her.

Matt had driven a circuitous route to arrive in the Wallowa Valley; there were no direct routes, and he had not trusted the condition of the unfamiliar back roads.

It had taken the better part of the day to arrive on the Oregon side of the Snake River. The mighty Kahmuenem of

Joseph's day was more subdued than it had been at the time of the Wallamwatkins's fateful crossing. On its far side they were soon within the traditional homeland of Joseph's band.

At dusk they had finally arrived at a park situated by a lake in the heart of the valley, and then, in full darkness, they overlooked that lake from a hilltop.

"I think we've chosen our spot wisely," Matt said softly to Katy.

She responded with a nod. In the distance the loftier mountain peaks rose majestically, bathed in moonlight. The scene was breathtaking, and Matt could feel a strong sense of identification for that beautiful land.

"On this night we will put to rest the unhappy spirit of Buffalo Robe," Matt continued. "And, little one," he said cupping her chin in his hand, "you too will find peace."

She nodded again, her large blue eyes unblinking, but he saw the shadow of a smile on her lips.

Matt looked once more at the shoreline below, half expecting to see the figures of his dream, hand in hand in their bridal attire; but in his dream they had appeared in full sunlight, and now it was night. In his heart, Matt hoped that by daylight their spirits would indeed find peace at last and fullfill the vision that had come to him along the Lochsa.

Katy had opened the satchel, and she handed him the shovel. "This is the spot," she whispered.

Matt began digging in the shelter of a pine on the bluff overlook. The ground was rocky, but he took his time. There were none to witness or object to his actions in that secluded spot.

When the opening was large enough, Katy spread a blanket on the ground and carefully placed the bones upon it. She knelt, and softly, in a chanting voice, she began the moaning death wail Matt had heard that other, more terrible time. As the cadence rose and fell, carrying across the air to the moon-dappled waters below, Matt placed the carefully wrapped bones in their grave.

Just before he began filling in the grave he saw Katy lift something from around her neck. It was the moss agate on its leather thong. Still on her knees, rocking gently back and forth with the rise and fall of her lament, she placed the owl amulet carefully within the folds of the blanket. Then her wailing subsided to a soft murmur. Matt gently replaced the earth and rock. He was reluctant to pile more rocks atop the shallow grave for fear of drawing attention to it. Instead, he smoothed the earth above it and restored its natural appearance.

When he had finished, Matt replaced the shovel in the satchel and knelt beside Katy. Her murmuring ceased as he put his arms around her and drew her to her feet.

She looked down on the restored grave and solemnly pronounced, "Now Buffalo Robe sleeps. His bones repose in the bosom of his earth mother in the valley that bore him and nurtured him. His spirit is free to roam in Ahkunkenekoo, the land above. We can do no more."

Then Katy's body was wracked with a violent trembling and her forehead began to perspire.

Matt grasped her shoulders and searched her face closely. "Katy, are you ill?" For a moment he remembered Doctor Langley's admonitions about her health, and he was frightened at the thought of all the emotional torment he had put Katy through in the past two days.

From the distant trees the descending call of a screech owl broke into the night. Matt was not surprised; he had come to accept the calling of the omnipresent creature, to believe in its symbolic guidance. He was more startled at the answering call of a coyote. From across the lake the cry wavered in the air, lingering like a prayer on the gentle breeze.

Katy closed her eyes and shook her head as if to clear

the conflicting emotions and thoughts from her mind. Then she looked at Matt, that time, miraculously, through the clear blue eyes of Katy Ketchum.

It was as though the calling of the owl and the baying response in the hills had signaled her release.

"Matthew Moss," she said clearly. Matt's heart warmed at the recognition. She was obviously in possession of herself once again. "Matthew Moss," she repeated, "I have been on a long, dark journey. I have seen many things previously unknown to me. I have looked into my heart and in it I discovered many things."

Matt looked at her with great tenderness.

"I have looked into your heart also," she said softly, "and I have seen your soul."

Matt was almost speechless with wonder. He had hoped, even expected, that when the bones were reinterred Katy would find release from whatever it was that had held such firm grasp over her. It was a miracle that he had her back, and he stood for a moment just looking at her. She was completely self-possessed and clear-eyed, beautiful in the moonlight. Her long black hair hung in thick braids below her shoulders, and Matt was touched by her beauty.

"You are whole again," he told her.

"I am whole." She looked deeply into his eyes. "You have shared my dark journey. Of that I'm certain. More than that, I feel an infinite sense of something spiritual having intervened, having guided me through this entire experience. More than that, I think something caused our paths to run a parallel course." She shook her head and laughed slightly. "But I'm a little bewildered. There are so many gaps in my memory."

Matt put his arm around her shoulders. "Come. Let's walk down to the lake. We can talk there. Maybe we can find a stump to sit on."

"Just like Moose Meadow Hill."

"Yes." He laughed. "You remember then."

They descended the bluff arm in arm. "Yes, I remember our meetings there, but my memory of the last day ends with the storm. I took the journals to the rock overlook above my camp that day in order to complete my reading. There was a sudden storm, as I'm sure you know. I managed to protect the journals in their box and to secure it under a sheltering ledge. It was when I went to retrieve my own notebook that the wind had blown from my grasp that lightning struck."

Katy shuddered slightly. "I'll never forget how it felt to watch that tree fall, knowing I would be under it when it struck the ground."

Matt drew her closer and gave her shoulder a reassuring squeeze. They stopped by the water's edge. A half-submerged tree lay in the water and Matt climbed out onto its trunk, offering Katy a hand to follow. They sat down side by side and gazed across the silver expanse of water.

Then Katy continued. "I remember twisting my ankle and falling against the rocks just before the tree struck." She shrugged her shoulders. "But that's my last conscious memory."

She leaned her head against Matt's shoulder while he filled in the details of her rescue. He minimized his role in saving her life, but Katy was aware of the dedication he had shown during the time that had elapsed since the accident.

Katy sat in silence for a moment when he had finished. Then she raised her head from his shoulder and looked deep into his eyes. "There's one more thing I must know. It may be painful for you."

Matt's heart missed a beat. "Richard?"

"Yes. Richard. I've a vague recollection of having seen him during my convalescence, but I remember nothing more."

Matt cleared his throat. "It may be just as painful for you, little one." He had lapsed back into the term of endearment he had used when she was neither Katy nor Takseen. He wondered how he could tell Katy the truth about Richard without either hurting her or being unfair to Richard.

"I informed him of the accident as soon as you were under doctor's care," Matt told her. "Richard expressed concern but was unable to make the trip to Mount Lewis immediately."

"But he did come later?"

"Yes. He flew up on a weekend. You were still unconscious and he stayed only an hour."

"There's something wrong isn't there, Matt?" For a moment the light went out of Katy's eyes. "What else happened?"

"I don't want to hurt you, Katy, but you must know the truth. Richard's mother was with him. She didn't enter your room, but while she waited in the hall with me she told me that everything was over between you and Richard."

Katy passed a hand across her eyes, then rested her forehead on the back of her hand. "It's funny that I'm not more surprised. It's almost as if I had expected this. Is there anything else?"

Matt picked up her hand and held it tight. "Then you don't remember this morning?"

She looked puzzled, then hurt, while Matt narrated the morning's confrontation.

"What will Richard do? Surely he won't file charges?" she asked when Matt had finished.

"I think I talked him out of that. But, Katy," Matt said softly, "I don't think you'll be hearing from him again. It's all my fault. . . ."

She held up a hand in protest. "Don't blame yourself. I'd rather have it all behind me, Matt. I've sensed this coming but I've blinded myself to the realities. Oh, I'll see him again, all right. But it will just be to tie up the loose ends."

Matt tried to conceal his elation. Despite her protests, Katy's pride had been hurt by the rejection. He was about to pat her shoulder in consolation when Katy startled him by throwing her arms around his neck and giving him a hug.

When she withdrew she said, "I feel so free. You must be bewildered by my behavior. I'm not so disappointed at his rejection as you might think. Really. Don't look so worried." Then, in a more serious vein, she looked into Matt's eyes and let her own eyes speak for her.

Matt forced back a sudden wave of shyness, struggling with the reticent backwoodsman within him that sometimes overcame his powers of speech.

"I love you, Katy," he said finally, taking her in his arms.

She turned her face up to him and felt the warmth of his embrace, responding in kind before she too answered, "I love you."

Katy, after her dark, solitary journey, was hungry for the warmth and affection that Matt lavished on her. She loved the strength of his nearness, and his kisses restored her sense of well-being. They lingered along the lake shore, savoring the physical awareness that grew between them.

20

"I know now, as clearly as if I had experienced it myself, that my great-grandmother Takseen escaped from the Bear Paw Battlefield with her brother Yellow Moccasin. Beyond that, I'm not sure how she managed to survive the winter before making her way back to Idaho, where she apparently met her husband-to-be, Sam Ketchum."

Katy was lying on her stomach across the bed in the room that Matt had obtained for them. Perched against the pillow was the open journal that Katy was searching through. Matt lounged in an easy chair close by. His heart was warmed by the love he felt for Katy as he listened to the account of Takseen's ordeal as it had been revealed during Katy's dark journey.

When she had at last recounted the Bear Paw surrender and Takseen's escape, Katy turned to the final pages of the second journal. She hoped they might reveal the final chapter of Takseen's experiences.

"Here it is," she said excitedly. "Let me read this part to you."

"Go ahead," Matt urged her.

She began, hesitating here and there over the illegible or water-stained parts, piecing together the final chapter of Takseen's life.

After the surrender, Takseen and her brother, Yellow Moccasin, made their way to the Old Woman's country, where they wintered with a band of friendly Sioux. The winter passed without Incident for them, but others among their People were not so Fortunate. In later years Takseen learned that some who had escaped from the Bear Paws were Murdered in Cold Blood for their rifles. The Assiniboins were responsible for some such acts. The Gros Ventres helped them kill and scalp other Nez Perce who appealed to them for refuge. Takseen's attending spirit must have kept close watch over her, for she found freedom among the Sioux during that first winter following the Surrender.

I wish to record here some statistics I have since heard regarding the Surrender. Whether or not they be Truthful, I cannot say. At the site of the Bear Paw Battle, it is said that the Nez Perce surrendered 1531 horses, 300 saddles, along with bridles and ropes and camp equipment. They were given to understand that 700 horses would be returned to them. The Arms they turned in were not worth the having.

Of all the Injuns who surrendered, 87 were men, 184 women, and 147 children. Most of the men were old and at least forty of them were wounded.

From all accounts and especially from Takseen's eyewitness story which I have heard from her over the years, I would judge the world has never seen the likes of the campaign Joseph and the other Nez Perce Chiefs led those white men on. For four months those Injuns trekked, bag and baggage, outrunning and outthinking those white fools on horseback, who were much better equipped and had no old people or Women and Children to slow them down.

There's one thought that comes to me from time to time. If I could write a happy ending to, the journey of Joseph's people, I'd do it this way. It's a fact that General Sherman was just finishing a tour of the Yellowstone Country at the time the Nez Perce were entering from the West. He was Chief of the whole United States Army at that time. If the Injuns had run across General Sherman and captured him, why they could have ransomed him for their whole beloved Wallowa Valley!

But there you have a happy ending made up by a Broken-hearted old man. Still and all, if that had come to pass, I, in all likelihood, would never have met the girl I came to Love and Cherish, the Wife of my happiest years, the Mother of our only Son, John.

Katy paused and Matt interrupted, "What about that, Katy? Do you know how Takseen and Sam Ketchum happened to meet?"

"Just a minute, I think he tells here." Katy was running a finger beneath a blurred line of writing, trying to decipher it.

While she studied it she told Matt, "Great-grandpa, from accounts Grandpa John told me, was a giant of a man with a full red-gold beard that glinted in the sunlight and a smile that had melted the heart of many a lass back East before he gave up civilization for the mountains. He had some education—enough to make him a respectable, if somewhat rambling, writer."

She sat up and crossed her legs, resting the journal in her lap. "Listen, I think I can make it out now."

When Spring came, Takseen and her brother made their way back to Idaho. They were unhappy not knowing what had happened to the Survivors. Takseen told me she had never trusted the White men's promises and therefore was not surprised to learn that her People had not been returned to Lapwai as promised. At that time Joseph's band was a thousand miles away in Kansas, where they suffered all manner of Disease. Malaria was common for those Injuns because their Bodies were used to a cool dry climate and they could not take the Humid weather of the bottomlands. Nor could they drink the muddy water of the Missouri without suffering great Sickness. It was there that Joseph's infant daughter, born during the Campaign, died of a fever. No Newborn baby survived the Harsh conditions. Seven years passed before those people were allowed to return to the Northwest. Then they were divided into two groups, the first Injuns arriving at Lapwai under military escort, the remainder sent to the State of Washington.

It is for the memory of Takseen that I keep this record. But Moreover, I wish to pay my Humble respects to the memory of Chief Joseph, who, I have just heard, died a short time ago, on September 21, 1904, on the Colville Reservation in Nespelem, Washington. It is believed that he died of a Broken Heart.

Katy closed the journal, marking the place with her finger. Her voice was husky when she said to Matt, "What a tragic story. I can't quite reconcile the events, especially the irony

of Buffalo Robe having lost his life on their wedding day."
She handed the journal to Matt. "You read for a while."

"Takseen did find fulfillment, you know," he suggested
as he opened the volume to the place where she'd left off.
"Your great-grandpa speaks in very tender terms of his devotion to her. Listen to this."

I was camped in the Bitterroots, doing some horse
trading with the Injuns when I first laid eyes on the girl.
She was traveling with two families of Pasloos Injuns.
They were living off the land, minding their own Business,
and hoping the White man's government would do the
same. There were two other girls about her age in the
group, and the minute I saw her, I knew she was different
than those silly squaws she was traveling with. I could
tell from her somber manner that she had seen more
suffering than one her age should have. She was a might
shy, but I got her to tell me her name, and she sure was
as slender as the willow that she was named for. Takseen
was her Nez Perce name, she told me, though the Pasloos
called her by another. She was a beauty too.

Her brother, who was a fine-looking boy about thirteen or fourteen at that time, protected her from any
Effort on my part to make her acquaintance. When I
learned of the Ordeal they had been through in the past
year, I could well understand the hate he felt toward all
White men. Takseen was different, though. She gave me
credit for being more Human than some of my White
Brothers, and we gradually became acquainted. I spoke
the Injun sign language and a smattering of Nez Perce.
Between us we picked up enough words to communicate.

It took some doing, and what went on in our hearts
and minds is too Private for me to set pen to, but she
eventually consented to marry me. I expect it was partly

that she had no one left but her brother, partly because marriage to a White man would give her Freedom from being forced onto a Reservation. But if she married me at first for those reasons, she soon learned to love me, and our Marriage came to be based on Mutual Love and Affection. I never minded telling her I loved her.

Well, it makes my heart ache to recollect those early days together. We settled in this very cabin that she helped me build on Moose Meadow Hill. We were poor in money, but rich in Love and blessed with the Bounty of the land. There was food for the hunting, and cash money now and then for furs. It was a quiet life. Occasionally we'd have a visitor in the person of her brother Yellow Moccasin. But he was a restless Injun and always slipped out as quick as he came.

In the Meantime, our son John was born, and he was a better Man for the Mixed background we gave to him. Maybe someday he'll read this journal. If he does, I expect it will give him great Pride in his Injun heritage.

Come winter, maybe I'll write some more about our life together. There's another task I must tend to just now. When I began this journal not long ago, Takseen, whom I have known these twenty-five or more years as Sarah, lay abed with a fever. It's run its course now. Today I buried her. Reckon I'll carve a marker for her yet today.

She welcomed the return to her earth mother and she lies now beneath the ground. Her spirit can dwell in the meadow that is on fire with fall foliage and her fever-wracked body can know peace at last.

If she still thought of her dead warrior from time to time, she gave me no cause for jealousy, and today I can rejoice with her that her spirit has joined Buffalo Robe's in Ahkunkenekoo, the Land Above.

Matt closed the journal and they sat silently for a moment, each lost in his own thoughts.

Matt was first to break the silence. He rose from his chair and drew Katy from the bed, his arms warm around her.

"I have my own interpretation of the events of this past month. In my heart I can't believe that everything that happened was coincidence." He tipped Katy's chin so that he could look directly into her eyes. "I've felt an overwhelming sense of affection for you since our first meeting. More than that, I feel I've always known you."

Katy shook her head in agreement. "There's much I can't explain by natural means—those dreams, the strange state I was in for those weeks, our mutual attraction and sensitivity to one another. I will never know for certain why all this came about as it did."

She looked steadily at him again. "For me it is enough to know I love you, deeply and truly."

Matt kissed her long and tenderly. Katy thought her heart would burst with happiness when Matt said to her, "We can put the spirit of the Winding Water forever to rest by fulfilling what to me seems inevitable." For a moment the old shyness passed over him like a barely perceptible ripple in a pond. "Katy, I love you. It would make me very happy if you'd consent to marry me."

There were tears in Katy's eyes, but they were tears of happiness, and Matt needed no answer other than the loving look and the kiss that she gave him.

He broke away from her embrace when a sudden thought struck him. "The package!"

He had nearly forgotten the package that Richard had delivered. Matt brought it from his overnight bag. While Katy slipped off the strings Matt explained what had happened.

"Your father was so worried while you were hopitalized

that, just to get his mind off of you, he busied himself with all kinds of projects. Apparently one of them must have been cleaning out the attic, because he found this among his father's effects."

"Grandpa John's?" Katy said excitedly. She tore off the last of the wrappings and then breathed softly, "Oh, Matt, look."

She tremblingly drew from the box a white leather garment. Dry cleaning had not entirely eradicated the rusty stains on the bodice, but it was still beautiful with its intricate pattern of beading and quillwork.

"Takseen's wedding dress," they said in unison.

Katy stood before the mirror and held the century-old garment to her. Then she turned to Matt with tears in her eyes.

"We've come full circle, haven't we, Matt?" she said softly. "I think Takseen would approve if this dress could serve its original purpose, don't you?"

Matt had tears in his eyes too, and as he studied Katy with the soft doeskin dress held to her, he was struck by her beauty. "It looks as if it were made for you, Katy. She'd be proud to have you wear it."